SILENCE AT SALERNO

Silence at Salerno

A COMEDY OF INTRIGUE

BY Francis Steegmuller

Holt, Rinehart and Winston   New York

Published simultaneously in Canada by Holt,
Rinehart and Winston of Canada, Limited.

Library of Congress Cataloging in Publication Data
Steegmuller, Francis, 1906–
Silence at Salerno.

I. Title.
PZ3.S8126Si [PS3537.T267] 813'.5'2 77-17937
ISBN 0-03-041641-8

First Edition
Designer: Joy Chu

Printed in the United States of America
10 9 8 7 6 5 4 3 2 1

Grateful acknowledgment is made for use of
portions of the following:

"Somewhere Over the Rainbow"
    Words by E. Y. Harburg, music by Harold
    Arlen. Copyright 1938, renewed 1966 Metro-
    Goldwyn-Mayer Inc. Rights controlled by LEO
    FEIST INC. New York, N. Y. Used by permission.

"Someone to Watch Over Me"
    By George and Ira Gershwin. © 1926 NEW
    WORLD MUSIC CORPORATION. Copyright renewed.
    All rights reserved. Used by permission.

"Easy to Love"
    By Cole Porter. Copyright © 1936 by Chappell
    & Co., Inc. Copyright renewed, assigned to John
    F. Wharton, Trustee of Cole Porter Musical
    and Literary Trusts. International copyright
    secured. All rights reserved. Used by permission.

Again, to Shirley

The characters and events in this novel are entirely imaginary. As for the setting, although there are actual islands in the Gulf of Naples that might have served, the author has allowed himself the pleasure of inventing an island of his own.

PART
ONE

1

Salt was scarce in Italy that spring. Nat Haley walked into one Salerno tobacco shop after another—those establishments being the licensed outlets for the twin state monopolies—and always met the same reply: "Niente sale. Sale niente." No salt.

He was on his way to see the temples at Paestum. From the island where he was staying in the Gulf of Naples, steamer schedules made a night's stopover at Salerno unavoidable; and it was for want of other distraction that, sauntering along streets crowded with evening shoppers, he thought of replenishing the salt that was low in his cupboard—his island tobacconist having already declared himself out of stock. Nat had supposed that to be a single, accidental case.

Here in Salerno there was no salt either, and none of the tobacconists seemed to know the reason, or to care. Most of them merely shrugged. "In Italy we've stopped asking why." One claimed it was because the blood of the local saint, dead these many centuries, had failed to liquefy in the annual ceremony in the cathedral. Finally, in an establishment more luxurious than the others, after the usual refusal Nat caught sight of a rare and expensive Turkish cigarette that he liked, and his buying a quantity made a difference. A very small package was whisked from under the counter and thrust at him. He left the shop feeling half-ashamed.

Nat was soon to think of that search for salt in Salerno as a prologue. The events which immediately followed surprised him the more because he was in a mood of non-expectancy, still numbed by loss—the loss of his wife, who had dreadfully sickened and recently died—and he had chosen his Italian island as a place of withdrawal. But only a few minutes later, back in the busy shopping street of Salerno, he ran into Melba Rovigliano, not seen in more than twenty years.

Nat recognized Melba at once. She was still petite and plump, pigeon-like, even more so now that her once black hair was silvery, a change that altered the emphasis of her features. Her printed silk dress, too, in a staid pattern of slate and white, Nat recognized as one she had worn at that time long ago. And she was still wearing it with much the same settled trimness he remembered.

As for Melba's equally instant recognition of Nat, it was peculiar. Nat saw that she was in an abnormal, agitated state. This was evident not only from her total lack of surprise at seeing him, but also from her obliviousness of his own great surprise. She ignored his exclamations, shook hands with him as though they had last met only yesterday, and asked quite abruptly where they could go and "sit down for a little talk." It was strange; she acted precisely as if they had made an appointment to meet that day in that street, in that town which was neither hers nor his. Whereas Nat's memory was that she almost never left the family house in Naples except for a few summer weeks at the Rovigliano villa on the slopes of Vesuvius, or for an occasional visit to a convent. Perhaps things had changed. And in fact Melba said at once: "You know my brother passed away?" Familiar with her family's story as he was, Nat suspected, murmuring condolences, that her air of being unhinged had its origin in testamentary complications.

It was a few minutes' walk to one of the cafés along the Salerno seaside, and before they reached it Melba was talking incoherently about the sound of rats behind her palazzo walls at

Naples and the blare of a jukebox overhead there, "although the members of the Club are really very polite." Her clearest statement was, "I had to get away if only for a few hours." Her rambling was partly in Italian, partly in English: thanks to Italian father, American mother, and English nanny, Melba and her brother had always been perfectly bilingual.

As a girl Melba had gone to boarding school at the Rome establishment of the French Sacred Heart nuns, the Dames du Sacré-Coeur, a long, low orange-colored building at Trinitá dei Monti, above the Spanish Steps. Nat's mother, who had attended an American convent boarding school, had once said something about "Sacred Heart girls": "They all have the reputation of not laying too much stress on sincerity. But most of the European ones I've met have a certain style." On being asked whether she could be more precise, Mrs. Haley, no femme du monde but an excellent maîtresse de maison, amended: "Let's say like a perfect French finish on a table." And indeed Melba's "French finish"—her subtle polish of manner—was apparent even today, when she was so uncharacteristically distraught. As for her sincerity ... Nat had once had occasion to notice a lack of it; but, as that lack had played a role in her helping him when she did, it would have been ungrateful to complain of it.

2

In what now seemed a previous existence, Nat Haley had become familiar with two episodes from American "cultural history."

Like anyone who had read a history of the Metropolitan

Museum of Art, he knew the story of General Luigi di Cesnola and the Cypriot sculptures. In the 1870s the Italian-born General was the Museum's first director, and the group of antique sculptures from Cyprus which he had acquired while American consul on that island formed the Metropolitan's first sizable collection of classical antiquities. To the astonishment of the Museum's trustees—that self-perpetuating body of wealthy businessmen, or "public-spirited art lovers," whose role it is to express "perfect confidence in the Director"—the exhibition of the Cypriot statues was the occasion for immediate scandal. Large numbers of ordinary New Yorkers were encouraged to believe, through articles in the press which professed to quote experts, that the sculptures were forgeries and that the General had in full awareness perpetrated the fraud for his own financial gain. (It was not known at the time that the "experts" were in the pay of a few vindictive millionaires whose "inferior social position" had caused them to be ignored by the "socially prominent" organizers of the Museum.) Eventually the sculptures were shown to be genuine, and the trustees' "perfect confidence in the Director" was thus triumphantly vindicated.

Nor was their confidence shaken, but rather confirmed, by a revelation made to them by the director during the intra-Museum investigation which the scandal provoked. Because the Turkish government had for reasons of its own decreed that the American consul was "forbidden to export antiquities from Cyprus," he had had the sculptures shipped out in packing cases marked "Property of the Russian Consul." In an after-dinner "confession" that was frequently interrupted by laughter and applause, the General told the trustees that he had "expressed his gratitude" to the Cypriot customs employees who had winked at the subterfuge. "Even with that slight added cost," he said, "I assure you, Gentlemen, that the Museum has a stunning bargain." "And a tip-top Director!" shouted one of the trustees. There were cries of "Hear, hear!" and the General responded with "Three hearty cheers for our dear New York Museum!" The trustee whose ungrammatical memoirs are the source of this denouement concludes: "After the meeting, when the Director had left the room and was safely out of earshot, one of our body expressed the feelings of us all: 'When Dago meets Turk, who's to speak of foul?' "

It happened that at this time a series of events resembling the story of the General and the sculptures was taking place in another American museum—the art gallery of "a Midwestern Educational Institution," as it was to describe itself on a later occasion when anonymity seemed desirable.

Neither Dagos nor Turks were involved in this deal. All passed among white Anglo-Saxon Protestants. On the one hand an unworldly nineteenth-century New Englander, son of a well-to-do Boston merchant, who from long residence in Florence had brought back a collection of early Italian paintings of a style then unfashionable; on the other, one of the Institution's professors and its inevitable board of trustees. In need of money and failing everywhere to sell his beloved pictures, the New Englander was offered a loan of a few thousand dollars on them by the Institution, repayable by a certain date. (Even that small loan was authorized by the trustees reluctantly, at the urging of a canny professorial curator.) The pictures were hung. For Americans of that day, when "Old Masters" meant reproductions of Raphael, Leonardo and Titian, those older pictures—works by Sassetta, the followers of Giotto, and their contemporaries—were ludicrous in their stiffness, and the press jeered at them as crude forgeries. When the New Englander couldn't redeem his loan, he innocently agreed that the Institution should arrange an auction of the pictures, to provide him with funds. The morning of the sale, the professorial curator, speaking for the trustees, surprised the very few assembled potential buyers by "reminding" them that bids would be accepted only for the collection as a whole—a condition hitherto unspecified. Of course no such bid was forthcoming—except from the Institution itself, which offered exactly the amount of the loan plus interest. The auctioneer cried "Sold!," the loan to the collector was marked "Paid," and over his anguished protests his pictures passed into the possession of the Institution. One of those midwestern trustees soon went on record, in *his* memoirs, as calling the purchase of the Jason Deming collection "the smartest bit of business in the history of any American museum"; and that boast, though ultimately eclipsed, held its own into the 1970s.

Taken together, those two episodes indicate how quickly the burgeoning American art museums adopted their prevailing codes of ethics. Perhaps their model was the Louvre, with its Italian pictures garnered by Napoleon's art vandals. The Jason Deming story had been pretty much forgotten when in the 1950s Nathaniel Haley, assistant professor in a well-known American university, wrote and published Deming's biography. During the year he spent in Italy gathering documents for the book he met Donna Millicent Rovigliano, Jason Deming's Neapolitan granddaughter, named for her American grandmother and known in her family as "Melba," whose assistance was in due course acknowledged in the preface.

To ordinary citizens, including his own brothers and sisters, the late Jason Deming's infatuation with old pictures had appeared as madness; and unquestionably there was something fanatical about his collecting. He had done it with money his widowed mother let him take as advances against his eventual share of his father's estate; and after her death the other children went to law, had the squanderer declared financially incompetent and themselves constituted as a family council, doling him out an allowance for the rest of his days. This was done with the approval of Deming's long-suffering and desperate wife, who cared nothing for pictures and who, as a result of the disastrous auction, was forced to run her household close to the bone.

Despite the virtual theft of his collection, and in the face of general incomprehension, Deming maintained his enthusiasm, continuing to study if not to collect, and during his later years he wrote several books on art and archaeology. In the last of them, completed shortly before his death in the 1880s, he confessed that he had encouraged the courtship of his only daughter by "a young Neapolitan nobleman" because the country house owned by the young man's family was close to a buried Roman villa which he hoped to excavate. The young nobleman, Riccardo Rovigliano, became Melba's father, and on his own father's death succeeded to the title of Duca.

Neither during his own dukedom nor that of Melba's brother, also Riccardo, was the buried villa excavated. The orchards that flourish in the volcanic soil of Vesuvius bear the best-flavored apricots in Italy, and the crops from the grove covering the Roviglianos' ancient site were too valuable to be sacrificed to archaeology. Melba and her brother had grown up hearing the constant lament that the family fortune, much diminished over the centuries, would long since have been amply restored had it not been for the trickery of the American Institution. Nat found Melba obsessed by the old story. For her the auction rankled as though it had taken place only yesterday, and she told him without reserve that her brother's marriage to a midwestern society girl, encountered as a Red Cross volunteer during the First World War, had been motivated, in turn, by hopes of recouping at least some of the financial loss close to the source.

Long before Nat appeared on the scene in the 1950s the American Duchess had left Naples. Her excuse had been Italy's role in the new war, but even when that role was reversed and peace declared she continued to live in her native North American city, not far from the guilty Institution, on one of the Great Lakes. When Nat arrived in Naples seeking documents, the Duca was trying directly and through lawyers to persuade his absent wife to augment the regular allowance she made him: an American bomb had damaged the Naples house; in his opinion American money should repair it, and the sum offered by the War Reparations Commission was insufficient. Supervising repairs, telephoning lawyers, writing letters to America, card-playing, riding, kept him, as he put it to Nat, "infernally busy." He displayed little interest in his American grandfather except occasionally to complain about the "old boy's genius for losing money" and dismiss him as "crazy." It was Melba who spent hours with Nat over papers in a dusty palazzo storeroom.

Her slight "insincerity" which Nat remembered from those days consisted chiefly in the pretense that she "adored pictures," that her longing for her grandfather's collection and her willingness to help Nat study its formation sprang from an inherent love of great art. Whereas it became quickly clear to Nat that she cared no more for pictures than had old Deming's wife, her namesake, and that she was helping him because of a greater obsession—family— of which the collection was a part. Ancestry was Melba's passion. She knew passages of the *Almanach de Gotha* by heart, as a lover of poetry might know Milton or Browning. Before meeting her, Nat had never heard of the Collegio Araldico, or the *Libro d'oro della nobiltà italiana*, which she cited constantly to place titled relatives in all degrees of cousinship. The connections that fascinated her seemed to be factual enough—over centuries the ducal Roviglianos had married into many equally noble families; but present-day relations with the world of republican Italy were slight. Crested New Year's cards and wedding announcements stood on the mantelpiece of the salotto, but there were almost no visitors. Melba and her brother, especially Melba, lived in semi-seclusion.

The lot of an unmarried Italian woman above a certain age is seldom brilliant, especially if she lacks independent means; and Melba had been left dependent on the Duca. As a young woman she had had a pretty voice and the dream of training it, but her father and brother laughed her out of that: in those circles one's daughter didn't go on the stage. The name Melba had been part of the taunting and teasing, the Australian soprano being then at the height of her career. "Melba" persisted as a family nickname, and Nat found something poignant in her asking that he too call her Melba. She liked "Millicent," she said, for its American family association; but in Italy, where *mille* means "a thousand," and *cento* "a hundred," the name sounded arithmetical, even suggesting a price on her head. In fact, several tentative offers of marriage had come to nothing for financial reasons, though there had also been, on the Rovigliano side, "difficulties about rank." She said she often thought of taking the veil. Nat wondered whether she was deterred from doing so by a belief that she must keep house for her brother, to whom she was closely attached. Nat found the Duca an empty, braying kind of man, atrociously selfish, who treated his sister like a drudge.

Now, MEETING MELBA in Salerno, remembering her ancestor-worship, he found himself contrasting that with his own thoughts, which these days sometimes flowed in the opposite direction: would a solitude such as his be less acute if it were not childless?

3

SITTING WITH NAT in the café garden, Melba was more coherent, and quite compulsively garrulous about the background of her presence in Salerno.

Following her brother's death, she said, his American widow had done something grotesquely offensive. She had come and literally sealed off part of the story occupied by the family in the Naples house—bricked up the several doorways leading to the largest room, the principal salotto. Into it she had first crowded a mass of objects gathered from various other rooms, all of them things relating to the family or long in the family's possession—portraits, photographs, busts, genealogical documents, tapestries, furniture, bric-à-brac—as though to say: "These are mine: if you thought of selling them, think again."

According to the marriage contract, on the Duca's death his property, and of course title, were to pass to the couple's oldest surviving son. If there were no sons, the title would become extinct and all was to go to the Duchess or her heirs. As it turned out, there was no issue, and it was found that the Duchess had taken so many mortgages on both the palazzo and the villa—as an American she had been able to retain greater financial independence than any Italian-born wife—that by far the major interest in them was already hers, and the Duca had little to leave her. His will contained a late proviso that Melba be permitted to live in the family quarters of the Naples house for the rest of her life, that she receive for herself the rents paid by the tenants, and that, should the Duchess or her heirs dispose of the house during Melba's lifetime, Melba should be paid the equivalent of whatever share had remained the Duca's at the time of his death. The Duca's lawyers told Melba that this paragraph had been inserted at their insistence, and warned her that should it be contested it would be interpreted by any court as a mere suggestion, lacking legal force; but that without it, being left totally unprovided for by her brother, she would have had to sue the Duchess or her heirs to obtain some minimal reserve from the estate, a reserve that the law would certainly, although after interminable delay, have allowed her because of close kinship. Better let any suing be done by the other side, should they choose.

So far, the only activity had been that startling arrival of the Duchess herself, a few days after the funeral. She had come to Naples alone, put up in a hotel, appeared at the house with a pair of workmen engaged for her by the hotel concierge, supervised them as they filled the room with the selected objects, watched while they closed off all access, paid them, and departed. During her visits to the house she had given Melba a few uncordial words and refused all offers of refreshment. She disappeared without saying good-bye.

"Live without it," the lawyers advised Melba when she reported that she was losing her salotto. "Make no fuss. Forget that it ever existed."

But Melba could not forget the salotto. Too many noises came through the walls. The American Duchess had forgotten about Neapolitan rats.

There in the seaside café at Salerno, Melba depicted a super-race of rodents. "The rats of Naples! As big as hares, as dogs! A special breed! Their bristling reddish fur! Their beady eyes! Their bright yellow teeth, so long, so sharp! Ugh! And the grinding noise they make as they chew! In my mind I see them swarming over the salotto, up and down the walls, gnawing at the precious pictures themselves!"

The precious pictures! Melba's inherited regret for Jason Deming's stolen masterpieces seemed to have persuaded her that the walled-up room contained a great collection like his. Whereas Nat knew what the Rovigliano pictures were: a few blackened ancestors, assorted religious daubs blistering in their frames, engravings stained and spotted by damp. And two or three reproductions, wistfully or resentfully cut from newspapers or magazines, of ex-Deming treasures hanging in the Midwestern Educational Institution. The only pictures of any interest were a pair of American Victorian "crayon portraits" of Jason and Millicent Deming, in matching oval frames. Although when the drawings were done both Demings had been in healthy middle age, they appeared here as funereal effigies, typical victims of that repulsive medium. More than once, Melba said, she had heard a shattering of glass behind the wall; Nat envisaged the two oval frames finally chewed through and giving way. Probably the portraits themselves were devoured, by now. Better so. He himself had photographed them; as the only extant Deming likenesses, they had served as illustrations in his book, casting their unique pall over every copy.

Until recently, the rats had been the worst noisemakers.

And until recently Melba had lived fairly well on the rents. For generations most of the house had been leased to a variety of tenants. It was a huge old stone block, built by an ancestor in what was then a fashionable thoroughfare, Via Lupo, and known as Palazzo Rovigliano. Now it was dilapidated, a tenement, though if you looked up at it from across the narrow street the façade was seen to be handsome: the stone-carved family escutcheon still in place above the portico, the family name cut in the lintel. But all that once noble quarter of Naples was today little more than a slum. All day and most of the night it rang with the cries of its inhabitants. The street-floor of Palazzo Rovigliano was a row of small shops selling cheap jewelry, drygoods, hardware, sausages, cheese, pasta; the old stables in the courtyard housed a tailor, a printing press, an upholsterer; what had been the coachman's lodging was now a turbulent kindergarten. The upper floors were divided into residential flats. The American bomb had pierced several stories and exploded, weakly, in the family's billiard room—a salon which the Duca, who had been captain in a cavalry regiment, had eventually restored as a club room for his fellow ex-officers. He and the members called it the Royal Cavalry Club, though such a name was officially forbidden by the new Italian republic.

Over their coffee in the café, Melba resurrected the party her brother had given to celebrate the opening.

"A dance! I recognized it from the first as dangerous. Why not just a sherry party? We still had good sherry in the cellar. I warned Riccardo: 'Remember, every one of those pensioners is old enough to have ridden to war on a horse, and the same goes for the wives.' He was furious with me; they were a valiant lot, could dance till dawn like himself, and so on. Of course he wasn't in good health at all by then, but the old couples could have danced a little if it hadn't been for the floor. The workmen had delayed; Riccardo wouldn't postpone the inauguration of his precious club. Oh! Those poor old people with their feet stuck in the wet varnish! Flies on flypaper! Their struggles to move! Their faces! The fiasco! The shame of it! The talk of Naples! Cartoons in the leftist press! People still laugh themselves sick about it."

Despite the disastrous inauguration, a number of pensioners used the club quite regularly at first, dropping in before lunch or after siesta to read newspapers and talk about other days. But the Duca soon had to disconnect a bell the old soldiers had been invited to ring whenever they wanted coffee sent up from the family kitchen—even in post-war Naples servants could strike—and the coffee turned out to have been the chief attraction. Attendance dropped off at once. One by one the remaining habitués deserted or died. Even before the Duca's own death the Royal Cavalry Club was extinct.

The room stayed unused for years. The rest of the palazzo needed constant repair. All rents were legally determined and couldn't be raised; even so, tenants whose pipes and ceilings deteriorated began to withhold their payments, and those that were made went for the settlement of workmen's bills. Eventually Melba rented out the club room to a different group of gentlemen.

Nat sensed a certain reserve in her references to the "new Club," as she called it. "The members are very courteous to me. They always call me Principessa. You know that has been customary in the palazzo. They're in some kind of business: they've never told me what. I only wish they didn't have the jukebox. It's directly over my bedroom, and their busiest hours are at night." There was a brief recurrence of the agitation she had shown in the street: "Sometimes I think I'll go mad. The rats keep chewing, though what can be left for them I can't imagine. I don't sleep nearly enough. Not nearly enough. Will the day ever come when I can live in peace?"

She was in effect the manageress of an apartment house,

office building and shopping center combined. She was constantly on call. She had come to Salerno by bus just for the change, and would now bus back to Naples. "How I would love to have one quiet night!" But she couldn't stay. "Now I have to catch my bus. God bless you. It's done me good to reminisce about old times."

They hadn't reminisced about old times. But Nat was lonely, and the encounter had rekindled his liking for Melba. "I'd be happy," he said, "if you'd spend the night in Salerno as my guest at the hotel."

"You *are* kind." Tears came to Melba's eyes: not just a film, but tears that overflowed and ran down her face. She touched them with a handkerchief. "You *are* kind. But no, I must be off."

And only now did she become aware, at last, that the meeting there in Salerno was, in fact, a surprising event. Emerging from her trance, she looked at Nat closely. An hour before, in the street, she had certainly "recognized" him; but as she talked and talked he had been less and less sure that she was seeing him. Not once had she addressed him by name; her monologue might have been directed to anyone she had once known. Now, after a long look, she finally spoke his name. It came out as an exclamation: "Professor Haley! Nat!"

Then they did exchange a few words about old times. She asked how he happened to be in a busy, unattractive place like Salerno. Where was he living? What had he been doing all these years? "Did you ever marry?" He told her of his wife and what had recently happened. Her condolences were pious. "Much comes back to me. I'm sorry there's no time. I had things to tell you about my brother and your book. And about the pictures. But I really must go. The bus will be leaving."

She refused to let him accompany her, and only turned once to wave. From where he sat he saw her standing for a few minutes beside the highway. Then the bus came and she was gone.

At the very end he had noticed that she was not immaculate, as in the past she had been. The old print dress was dusty and dirty. Walking back to the hotel, in his mind's eye he saw reddish stains on the white parts of the pattern. It was sad to see old Deming's granddaughter too poor, or too distracted, to keep her dress clean.

4

THAT NIGHT there was a near-fatal accident at a table close to Nat's in the hotel restaurant. A party of Americans had come in for dinner, and one of the men almost choked to death on a piece of steak.

He had seen the group earlier, as he walked back along the waterfront after watching Melba go. They were a middle-aged half dozen, roistering on the afterdeck of a motor yacht that was tied up at the marina, GATTOPARDO II PALERMO lettered on the stern. All were nautically costumed to the point of travesty; there were shrill cries to the clink of ice and the blare of a transistor. One of the women hailed him as a fellow citizen and potential pal: "Join us for a martooni! What about a tooni?" Nat called thanks, but pointed to his watch and to the hotel and made the telephone-dialing sign as indication of urgent business.

In the dining room the hilarity the three couples brought with them gave way to a sound of gagging, which silenced the rest of the room and grew louder and more agonized; there was a contorted red face, there were men on their feet, waiters were running; a woman's voice cried, "My God, you can die that way!" A man was hauled choking from his chair, turned upside down, stood on his head, pounded back and front; then a crescendo of retching and the favorable outcome announced by cries of "Atta boy!" and hand-clapping. The near-victim, right end up again, was half-carried from the room, and a woman's voice was heard again above the relief of resumed talk: "Harry always did talk too much while he was eatin'."

The next morning, at Paestum, when Nat was reading about the rape of the Greek city by the mountain people—400 B.C., the guidebook said: he found he was sitting on "the capsized stones of the Temple of Neptune"—the now recognizable American chorus rose around him, and the *Gattopardo* people, today in Madras shirts and nylon pantsuits, erupted through the rows of fluted columns. "This is it, definitely!" "Home sweet home!" "Girls, this is the scene!" And one of them, Harry the choker, addressed Nat directly in a voice happy enough, if hoarse: "Pardon us: you don't know it, but you're sitting on our bunks." There was no question of being excluded from the exultant reconstruction of the scene of a generation earlier: these men were heroes, veterans, survivors, from the American Sixth Army Corps who camped in the Paestum temples after the 1943 Salerno landings. "We were so dumb in those days we supposed it was the Krauts had rooned the place," said Harry. "Jesus, I was nineteen." Now they knew better—the girls had read up for the trip; Sicily had been "fabulous" (one man had done some of his fighting there): this was the first stop since setting out on the yacht hired in Palermo. They were having trouble sorting out Palermo from Salerno. Soberly: "We plan to see many places of interest." Anzio, up the coast, would be the high point of the cruise—there were buddies' graves in the military cemetery there they wanted to visit: "They say they're kept up nice."

Pietas!

Before lunch, they would visit the site of the beachhead itself. It amused them that the *Gattopardo II* hadn't been able to bring them all the way: "Paestum has no landing facilities," its skipper-owner had told them. They laughed. "Now they tell us. In '43 we waded ashore." Today they had motored down, like everyone else, from Salerno. And from the temples it would be only a few minutes' drive, about a mile, to the site of the beachhead. The new brevity of their everlasting pre-dawn walk under German fire brought grim smiles. "Not a scratch," one of them said, belligerently. "Never a scratch." Nat wondered whether Harry, at least, might have some feeling that he'd been pushing his luck, coming back.

The skipper suggested that at Anzio they "park the yacht" and spend a day and a night sightseeing in Rome. The boat had been chartered for only a week, but now the skipper was urging them to sail further north, promising them a galaxy of military cemeteries as far up the coast as Genoa. However, "We aren't familiar with the situation up there; we figure he may not be, either—just greedy for the dough."

There was an exchange of names and hometowns. On hearing where Nat was at present living, the men showed animation: "Remember? That island was officers' territory—a rest spot for the brass. Is it still exclusive?" And when reassured: "Maybe we could fit it in after the graves."

As they said good-bye, Nat saw the two cars they had come in, each a Mercedes, with Salernitan chauffeurs, waiting outside the gate of the temple enclosure, to take them all to the beachhead, back down the lucky mile.

5

SHORTLY AFTER the publication of *Jason Deming*, now almost twenty years ago, a note from the departmental secretary had requested Assistant Professor Haley to seek an appointment with a person seldom seen, in that pre-revolutionary era, by lesser members of the faculty—the president of the university. Nat did so, and there followed one of those rare half hours that change a life for the better.

The president announced that he had received a "very disturbing" letter from his "very good friend" the president of the Midwestern Educational Institution, calling the book to his attention and asking whether he didn't agree that—the president then read aloud—"the tone of the references to the acquisition of the Deming pictures is offensive in the extreme, and might suggest that this member of your faculty undervalues commonly recognized academic standards of decorum." "I don't quite know how to reply," the president said. "I shall of course point out that the book wasn't published by our own press. Nevertheless, we had accepted it as your doctoral thesis, and thus are to a considerable degree culpable."

"Culpable?"

"Unquestionably. I have read the passages at issue, and wish I had seen them before publication."

"Straight accounts of events which took place, with quotations, including some self-congratulations, from the participants themselves."

"That may be. In fact, precisely. In the context of the academic mystique, straight recounting may not be the most appropriate method of communicating scholarly data, especially when it involves a fellow institution." The president paused grandly. "You are not, after all, a reporter."

But the great man did not, he said, want to be too hard on a member of his team; he had consulted with the chairman of Professor Haley's department, who was himself deeply concerned, and they agreed that if Professor Haley would write a letter which the president could pass on to his good, and learned, middlewestern friend, a letter conveying regret and the assurance that in future printings the offending passages would be revised, the matter might be considered closed. "As I scarcely have to point out to you, Professor Haley, the revisions would doubtless never have to be made. We all know that theses, or books made from them, are unlikely to have future printings. A conciliatory gesture . . ."

"Excuse me, Sir, but there is to be a future printing."

"What? What's that?"

It so happened that a paperback house had proposed to issue its own edition of *Jason Deming*—the thesis, or ex-thesis, having aroused a certain interest in the wider world of the arts. The typeface would be different—a circumstance, the editor pointed out, which would give Professor Haley the opportunity to revise the text if he wished. "And in any case, Sir, I'm afraid I couldn't write the kind of letter you suggest."

" 'In any case,' Professor Haley? Then *I* am afraid . . ."

The president hesitated. Neither his own thesis nor any of his subsequent publications had ever seen a "future printing," and that was hardening his heart against this assistant professor. On the other hand, he resented his good friend's impertinence, and could not wish to give him too much satisfaction.

The assistant professor solved the dilemma in words which until that moment he had had no conscious intention of uttering. "Don't concern yourself, Sir. I was about to resign anyway. It has little to do with the present detail."

"But Professor Haley . . ."

There was no reconsidering. And it was what the president, with his patronizing "after all," had reminded him he was not, that he in fact became: a reporter. Reporter, journalist, editor, and yet from time to time again the author of scholarly volumes. He was grateful to both presidents. Together, the censor and the trimmer had roused his spirit, given him the élan to break out of a community. Actually, though it would never have occurred to him to use the term, he was in a quiet way a kind of anarchist, tolerating only voluntary associations. He was insufficiently doctrinaire for the academic profession, at least as it was practiced today; the opinions he held were often unsettled or in conflict with each other.

AT PRESENT, in Italy, he was seeking recuperation from the loss he did not wish to talk about. He had fled New York, friends—especially those who kindly volunteered that "it would pass"—the telephone, the lunch tables, the editors and publishers in their offices. The Mediterranean island he traveled to was one he had not visited before. Nor was Paestum a place he knew. But he had always felt a certain harmony between himself and the ancient past, and now he was taking refuge in that. His wife had been a peculiarly vital spirit, and in the strange void she had left he was finding a degree of comfort in what Wordsworth called

> . . . evidence of monuments, erect,
> Prostrate, or leaning towards their common rest
> In earth, the widely scattered wreck sublime
> Of vanished nations.

Already, however, without realizing it, he was beginning to find that insufficient; but was still far from being ready to replace what he had lost with anything resembling it. He knew he wouldn't stay in this region of the mind or the globe forever. The island was a place of stopover, just as his spirit was at present set apart. Something would call him back. But as the weeks passed he still felt he had just arrived.

6

Sailing back from Salerno in the radiant afternoon, he thought of Melba in her crumbling quarter of Naples. Even though she "had things to tell him," there had been no suggestion that he visit her in the palazzo. Doubtless she was too harassed; and perhaps pride, too, kept her from inviting him. He wondered about the present aspect of the old house. The family rooms had never been the brightest in the world; now they could only be shabbier, like poor Melba herself. He imagined the salotto, tomb-like behind the Duchess's bricks and aswarm with rodents.

His own final view of the salotto, Nat recalled, had been on one of his last days of work in Naples and from a ladder—a long, shaky one brought in by a boy apparently no more than ten years old. There was the ladder, and there was a feather duster; and there were the boy and Melba. "Now climb the ladder, Pasquale, and dust the portrait, and then we'll do the same with the other one so the Professore can photograph them both."

"Sissignora."

But halfway up the quivering ladder Pasquale turned as white as his jacket, backed hastily down, and rushed for the door, his hand to his mouth; and in the doorway collided with the Duca, dressed for riding, and vomited not over his own jacket but over the Duca's. Nat remembered how the Duca, a large man with a great beak of a nose—there was no physical resemblance between brother and sister—had quickly pinched his nostrils shut with one hand and with the other struck the boy and cursed him, and shouted at him to "get out of here and go back to the peasant hut you came from," and followed that by more shouting, this time at Melba, abusing her for trying to make a house servant out of a bumpkin who should have been "left in the country with the apricots"; at which the boy burst into tears and sobbed, "Thank you, Signor Duca; you understand—it wasn't *nausea*, it was *nostalgia.*" Immediately the boy was patted and consoled by Melba and told not to worry, just to go and bring hot water and a rag. And then it was Nat who was urged not to worry—urged, that is, by the Duca not to think for a moment that the jacket, which he now dropped on the floor, might be ruined. He called Nat's attention to details of the reeking garment that identified it as a genuine Royal Cavalry coat, tailored from a marvelous material no longer manufactured, "adapted to all kinds of possible soiling by horses." Cleaning was advisable merely because "the odor of matter originating in a stranger might confuse the horse." And even before the boy returned with towel and basin the Duca abruptly changed the subject and made one of his few contributions to the project of the biography: "Before this photographing goes any further, Professor, let's clear one thing up, shall we? What do you think—would fifty dollars be a proper permissions fee?"

In the end it was Nat himself who climbed and moved the ladder for dusting and photographing the high-hung hideosities. Flakes, veritable pads, of clotted dust dropped to the floor. Melba apologized for Pasquale's rawness. He was just thirteen, up from the country. She and her brother were planning to improve his prospects. He was a bright boy. Her words were accompanied by a certain look, very fleeting, which Nat nevertheless recalled when the boy reappeared with dustpan and broom and he noticed that from the small face the nose jutted out in what was decidedly a beak.

On the steamer that afternoon from Salerno, he wondered whether there was anything to that conjecture, and where Pasquale might be now. The legal rights of illegitimate children in Italy were minimal. The tradition among the poor was to sentimentalize over them as infants, pet them, call them "children of the Madonna." But, for anything more substantial, a Pasquale needed a Melba in his life.

7

Bᴀᴄᴋ ᴏɴ his nearby island that evening he found his white-haired bachelor landlord, Signor Sacca, sitting on his flowery terrace with his sister and housekeeper, Immacolatina.

Immacolatina, a stout motherly spinster, was knitting as usual. She was always knitting garments of various sizes for cousins and the children of cousins: the tribe of Saccas had been islanders for generations, and generations on the island tended to be large ones. The several brothers and sisters of Nat's two Saccas had all emigrated to North America, and Nat supposed that the house name, Villa Bklyn, painted on a tile beside the two bells at the street gate, commemorated the absent ones and the return address as written on some of their envelopes. (The contraction, as applied to the gate post, resulted in some strange local pronunciations.) The top floor of Villa Bklyn had been remodeled into a separate flat. Having been careful to list it officially as an integral part of his own quarters, Sacca was able to rent it out for short terms only: as he hadn't hesitated to put it to Nat, he could legally "evict anybody he disliked." Nat had taken it as a sign that his own probation was more or less over when Immacolatina one day urged him to buy a television: she and her brother were worried about his sitting up there alone night after night "reading his eyes out."

Invariably the Saccas addressed him as "Professore," though not from knowledge of his academic past. In Italy Professore is a title easily given to any male of respectable appearance seen reading, or even carrying, a volume other than a comic book.

Once a week Immacolatina cleaned Nat's flat, and sometimes she cooked him a meal in his kitchen. Now he showed her the salt he had brought back from Salerno and told about his search. "Why such a tiny package?" Immacolatina asked. "I noticed you were running short. I'll get you a proper quantity tomorrow."

"You must be a privileged character at the tobacconist's, then. They said no to me."

"Tobacconist's? There's no salt anymore at the tobacconist's."

"Then . . . ?"

Immacolatina replied mutely, with a movement of hands and shoulders out of the region's gesture-repertory that had come down from antiquity but which Nat had not yet learned to interpret. Sacca gave a rough laugh. "You know why those Salernitani 'didn't know' why there's a salt shortage, Professore? I'll tell you. Because the Salernitani are worse liars than the Napoletani. And you know what that means. Liars! Cities of liars, both of them! *All* of them! The Romani, too. Liars! All liars!"

Given to tirades, which could turn his normally red face purple, Sacca was now well on his way.

"Everybody else in Italy knows why there's no salt, Professore. The government keeps the story out of the newspapers, of course. But everybody knows. It's because the workmen in the salt refineries are on strike, Professore! The state salt monopoly is due to be abolished. Next year salt will be a free commodity, as in civilized countries. Like even Sicily! Like even Sardinia! Imagine, Professore! Even on those two miserable islands, due to some old law, salt is sold freely, like butter and eggs. And next year it will be so everywhere in Italy. Except that I can't believe it will ever happen, Professore: that would be much too civilized for this poor peninsula. The refinery workers are civil servants, Professore. They see their work coming to an end, and they're on strike against the government, demanding the promise of a pension, or a year's pay at the very least, when the monopoly is abolished. The government says no—it promises it will 'absorb' them all, every last salt man, into other branches of the civil service. Imagine! Absorbing salt men! Where? Who would trust government promises anyway? The refiners are on strike, Professore. That's why there is no salt."

"But . . ."

Hadn't Immacolatina just said she would buy salt tomorrow? She was smiling now, smiling into her knitting.

And Sacca, still excited, was talking about something else. He was announcing that the night before, while Nat was in Salerno, the swimming pool of the Grand Hotel Imperatore, the most fashionable hotel on the island, had been wrecked by vandals. Expertly wrecked. Explosives had been used in the pool and on the pump system. Sacca said it was the worst episode of local violence since the British and French exchanged fire on the cliffs during the Napoleonic wars. Those Anglo-French skirmishes were the last time anyone on the island except hunters had shot to kill. In the Imperatore incident no one had been killed or even hurt, but "We are very different from those other islands, Professore, where salt may be free but life is cheap."

The island was indeed much vaunted, in travel brochures and by its own inhabitants, as a haven of peace. One aspect of this peace struck Nat as singular, however. A number of the island's privately owned grottoes, opening directly from the sea, had become fueling stations for the "spiders," the tiny, lightning-fast black motorboats used by Neapolitan smugglers to take delivery of contraband goods from vessels far off in international waters—opium and cocaine from Turkish and South American freighters, cigarettes and whiskey from American naval craft. Almost every day one could see a squadron of half a dozen spiders dash toward the horizon and disappear, leaving long white parallels of wake;

later in the day they would return in the same formation. A police helicopter might be hovering as they approached the shore. Sacca explained that the helicopters, from the government air patrol, were checking the number of spiders in action each day, and sending the figure by radio to the Neapolitan harbor police. The spiders carried their cargoes to Naples by night; the police were waiting; in the dark a satisfactory financial arrangement would be made and the goods landed. The owners of the fleet, a group referred to by Sacca merely as "the Consortium," took care of any employees found to be cheating. Occasionally the body of one of them would be found floating near Naples. The island itself remained at "peace." "The whole thing is a model of how an operation should be run," Sacca said. On the subject of the spiders, he was at once sardonic and admiring. Nat knew that he owned various properties on the island. Perhaps a grotto or two was among them.

8

WHEN NEWLY ARRIVED on the island, Nat had stayed for a time at the Hotel Imperatore; and near noon of the day after his return from Salerno he exchanged greetings with the white-haired, white-jacketed personage with epaulettes of gold braid who was taking the air among the as yet empty tables on its streetside terrace. This was Mario, sovereign of the Imperatore's bars. He too was a recent widower, and from discovery of each other's state a sympathy had sprung up between them. Today it occurred to Nat, as he saw Mario's change of expression, that this elegant maggior-domo was the opposite of Signor Sacca: his customary manner was one unruffled by any action that he might witness on the world's stage. That professional veneer cracked slightly this morning at the exchange of greetings: Mario knew what Nat was thinking—that this was not his usual post at mid-day in late spring. His warm-weather kingdom was the garden bar, behind the hotel, close to the pool. Now he made a slight backward move of his head, recognizable as an invitation, and ushered Nat through the lobby onto the rear terrace, where a few guests were staring at the wreckage. "Dynamite," he said.

The Imperatore's garden was devastated: flooded by water, now subsiding, that had poured from shattered pipes; littered with concrete fragments of the pool which workmen, barefoot in the mud, were removing in wheelbarrows. The culprit or culprits—one, at least, had known that the pool was emptied Thursday nights, to be cleaned for weekend bathers—had placed a charge beside the pump cabin and another in a hole pickaxed inside the pool itself; he or they had lit the fuses and fled. The blasts had been dull; no one had been fully roused. The night watchman was under no definite suspicion of collaborating, but was being held in the local jail anyway: in his alibi he had eagerly confessed to leaving the hotel and its garden to spend several hours in a local bar, where he had been invited by "a very minor member of the staff," as Mario put it. On his return he had found a comfortable corner and slept it off. That was all that was known, and Mario was disinclined to offer his own speculations or to repeat those of others. He soon excused himself to return to duty: detectives flown from Rome in a police seaplane were at this moment on their way from the harbor to have lunch before launching investigations, and his bar would undoubtedly be their first stop.

As Nat moved off toward the beach he passed them—a trio of unmistakables, escorted by several island officials, among them the local Commissario, or Chief of Police.

9

I⊤ was a beach in a manner of speaking. The island shore, chiefly grottoes and rocky coves, was only here and there edged with pebbles. The Cala, as this inlet was called, had no such rim; one plunged into the sea from the rocks, or let oneself down the ladder alongside the jetty. The jetty was modern, but since antiquity the Cala had been one of the island's smaller ports; underwater you could see a portion of Roman seawall, still retaining a pair of its iron mooring rings. The prospect as you looked out to sea was of needles and islands of rock rising sheer out of deep water; coastlines spaced with old watchtowers. The touristic and industrial developments further south, toward Salerno, were too distant to be seen from the island, but the pollution they caused was another matter: there were times at the Cala when a floating carpet of garbage or a film of oil forbade bathing.

But this was a good day: the water was so clear that as Nat looked down on it from above, painted small craft and their red and orange mooring buoys seemed to hover in bright air. He went lightly down the last steps, undressed behind rocks and swam to one of the buoys: floating, you looked up into an infinite blue glare, with a near-circular peripheral vision of clifftops white with sun and the droppings of gulls. Only to buoys and boats and their lines was it possible to hold: rocks and cliffsides were slippery with sea moss or spiked with barnacles and sea urchins; he rested at the buoy, the globe bobbing as he held, and swam slowly back.

Someone else had come to the Cala. Somebody was hailing.

"Dottore! Professore!"

The hailer was waving. A tall, slim, bronzed figure in a tiny red bathing slip. The accent was American, the tone bantering. And the face, when at last discerned, familiar to Nat.

Most of Nat's working associates were ignorant of his previous profession or indifferent to it; but occasionally someone enjoyed being tiresome. Such was Lyle Brennan. Some years before, as colleagues on the vast staff of a New York newspaper, they had seen each other daily; and here was Lyle standing among the island rocks calling out the honorifics it had pleased him to use then: "Dottore! Herr Doktor! Professore!"

And when Nat climbed out of the sea and joined him, Lyle's greeting was: "How goes the Psychographer?"

Nat knew the implications of "psychographer," a self-ennobling term coined by a pretentious, now defunct biographer of the 1920s. Lyle was probably using it with particular reference to *Jason Deming*, though his banter was doubtless aimed more broadly, at Nat's work in general, publications usually included in rather solemn "recommended" lists but never best sellers: the opposite fate from that of the single book Lyle had produced—a novel about his own cousin which had made him rich and almost as celebrated as the cousin herself. That had happened since he and Nat had last met. In magazines, Nat had seen photographs of the villa on the Venetian lagoon where Lyle now spent much of his time.

"And you, Lyle? Still a Naturalist of Souls?" That was another term favored by the 'twenties biographer. But Nat knew from experience that sparring with Lyle was best avoided: his ripostes were apt to grow barbed; you had to be careful if his company was to remain tolerable. Too careful, for Nat's taste. He asked what Lyle was doing on the island.

"What am I doing? You know me: I'm involved in a situation."

What now? A sugarplum from Lyle's "private" life? Following the triumph of his book, he had achieved television notoriety, notably through being interviewed in a series of "Confessions," billed as taking full advantage of the "frankness" and "honesty" now permitted in the medium.

But as Lyle presented it, today's "situation" was non-priapic. "It's a coincidence running into you, Nat. I'm toying with the idea of following in your footsteps—writing about the past. Not about yesterday. I've done yesterday. The past. A novel dealing with characters long dead."

"Real characters from the past?"

"A real one. Historical."

"May I ask who?"

"There was a medieval queen of Naples named Matilda. . . ."

"Matilda the Merciful." A legendarily pious and long-suffering member of the same ancient dynasty which Nat had often heard Melba Rovigliano claim as her family's forebears. More particularly, he recalled, the Roviglianos were supposedly in direct line of descent from a cousin and successor of Matilda's, a certain very pugnacious King Ladislao. "You're visiting the scene of her exile?" Matilda, deposed by relatives, had ended her days in the keep of the island's clifftop castle, now a casino. "Wasn't she accused of murdering her first husband?"

"Yes, by poisoning, my dear fellow, by poisoning!" Lyle seemed to relish the detail. "You can't say I lack variety in my plots. My last heroine's first husband, if you recall, died quite differently."

Lyle being as he was, Nat was forced to suspect that the unlikely "situation" involving an ancient queen of Naples (the fact of her having had a first husband who met with sudden death suggested itself as the sole reason for Lyle's having heard of her) had been invented as a springboard to some matter of more genuine concern. This could scarcely be unconnected with Lyle's own career. Further self-reference might now be expected.

Several years before, Lyle had had the shrewdness to see in his cousin Julia, born Brennan, a ready-made heroine for a novel. As the wife of a rising young statesman perhaps destined for eventual presidential candidacy, she had been conspicuous in and out of Washington for her beauty and her intensely publicized variety of roles—political hostess, best-dressed woman, mother of seraphic-looking children; in her bereavement following her husband's death in a plane crash she had received the condolences of the nation; then she had married again—this time, money: money that so dominated the famous, tight-lipped little old man who had made it that he appeared, scarcely personified, as a mere assemblage of interlocking multinational directorships. In appearance she and Lyle were alike—the same leonine head of thick tawny hair, the same slanting green eyes; the same configuration that could be photographed to suggest anything from mad gaiety to brooding introspection. Lyle's novel had been advertised as "compassionate," showing how his heroine, the only child of a financier father, had become embittered by his conviction and imprisonment for fraud during the Great Depression. An ambulance-chasing publisher had brought the book out immediately following Julia's real-life money-marriage—the step that instantly transformed her, in the public's eye, from one kind of heroine to another.

More reportage than imagination had gone into Lyle's narrative. Nationally known characters, their names more or less changed, were recognizable in an avalanche of "inside" detail: as a journalist, Lyle's specialty had always been gossip.

Nat pretended to take seriously the project of the Neapolitan queen. "There are all kinds of guidelines to Matilda. She left innumerable traces. The archive about her must be very rich."

"Professor, do my antennae tell me you're suggesting research?"

"Mightn't some be necessary?"

Lyle seemed to forget that it was he who had first mentioned historical study. "Oh, of course I'd have to read up. Establish the main outlines. But deep research, Herr Psychographer, deep research . . ." And there followed the litany, familiar to scholars, of the "creative artist" who is too intuitive to grub for details: "deadly

... counter-creative ... stifles the imagination ... there's such a thing as too many facts ..." and a final flick: "... murderous to sales, as you yourself must know."

Nat's recent intimacy with destruction of a body and mind had eroded his will to work; now Lyle's gibes brought momentary nostalgia for the discipline—immersion in pictures and books and manuscripts, hunting for the unknown and the missing in old galleries and libraries and the bright luxury of modern museums and "research centers," conversations, letters sent and received, the assimilation of others' thoughts; enlightenment that came gradually or in flashes; the game of sifting fact from myth while giving myth its due; and, in the writing, trying to bring order out of chaos while keeping paradox alive.

Lyle's little candle to Matilda was flickering badly. "I don't know, though. Any book about people in the past, novel or otherwise ... I'm not sure I'd want to bother. A book like that comes to a dead end. It's written—finished—and then what? Nothing happens. I don't mean prizes. I know you've had prizes. But such books are just monuments, really. Gravestones. I need a living sequel."

Certainly none of Nat's books had aroused the hullabaloo that had greeted Lyle's fiction about his cousin. Public denial on both sides that anything had been taken from "real life," and smiling photographs of the two of them, arm in arm, had littered the news. (They both had large mouths and splendid American orthodontia, and could smile treacherously and tremendously.) Then, as millions read the book and as gossip about its "truth" poured from the columnists, all the media broadcast Lyle's regret, his sorrowful wondering why he had in consequence become persona non grata to this much-loved cousin, childhood playmate and dearest friend.

"Of course," Lyle now added, "with your kind of book I don't suppose you worry about that sort of thing, because you can't expect it."

"That sort of thing" was presumably the required "living sequel"—whatever Lyle meant by that. Was he referring to the rumpus over his roman à clef? Surely a new life, a life more to one's liking than the old, which was what *Jason Deming* had brought Nat after the presidential rebuke, might be considered as much a living sequel? Perhaps not, in Lyle's view. In any case, Nat disliked the turn the talk was taking. Change of site might change the subject, and he proposed that the two of them leave their rocks and lunch on a pizza and a glass of wine.

10

Being hard to reach except by boat and even harder to leave—it lay at the foot of a long rugged path cut in the face of a cliff—the Cala was not popular with tourists, and had stayed simple. The few bathhouses could be rented or done without, and their concessionaire stoked his pizza oven on demand. As Nat and Lyle sat at table under a thatch roof, the salt shortage came up almost at once.

It began with Lyle's saying that at his Venetian villa he swam in his own pool, in seawater electrically pumped and filtered. "To get the permits I had to slip presents to a dozen officials, and it's costing me a fortune to maintain. There's one preposterous item— my annual tax bill from the Italian state salt monopoly for the salt in my swimming water."

On his way to table Lyle had stopped at his bathhouse for a flowing coral-colored caftan, an elegant garment of a kind uncommon on the island: it suggested the style of life in his villa, described in magazine captions as "sybaritic."

"The salt monopoly prepares its bills in connivance with the electric company, also state-owned. From the pump's meter-reading they figure the cubic yardage of water pumped. Divide by the supposed salt content per cubic yard, multiply by the price per kilo of salt, apply the tax rate, and mail the bill. They cheat madly about the salt content, of course. They seem to figure it at about ninety-nine and nine-tenths percent: the Dead Sea and the Great Salt Lake are pure springwater in comparison."

"I gather you won't be getting salt bills much longer." Nat reported what Sacca had said about the approaching end of the monopoly.

Lyle expressed little interest in that: perhaps facts took on the tedium of research when related by anyone except himself. He went on: "There's something *about* salt. A friend from home tried to bring me in a box of American salt a few weeks ago. When the customs people saw it and he tried to dicker with them he had the impression it would have been easier to import pure heroin. They said they'd have to confiscate it. But he said oh no, he hadn't brought it for their use. He's deliciously fey, and made a scene of dumping it, swirling the salt onto the floor right there, like a sand painting or a Pollock. Everybody was scandalized. They called the Carabinieri, but finally let him go."

"Why a salt monopoly in Italy anyway? In countries where salt is scarce, fair distribution might call for supervision, but why here?"

"Because anything to do with salt is crazy. Dr. Ernest Jones goes into that. Have you read Dr. Ernest Jones on salt? He confirms many things I've observed myself. Salt does things to people. To their minds."

Salt also, apparently, made strange bedfellows. Nat concealed his surprise at hearing Dr. Ernest Jones mentioned with approval by Lyle Brennan.

"Do you know that to this day the lagoon people around me go much further than just throwing spilled salt over their shoulder to hit the devil in the eye, as they say? A saltcellar at their table is never handed by one person to another. It's only moved within reach, to be picked up by the person wanting it. Some old taboo lingers on."

Nat had noticed that on the island money usually changed hands in that way—laid down, to be taken up by the recipient. If there was salt magic about, might it have played a role in the Salernitan shopkeepers' reluctance even to discuss the salt question?

"I've come to look on my swimming-water tax as just an up-to-date bit of the old salt craziness." Lyle told more about the "lagoon people." How he had discovered that their fertility pill was a bath in salt water; that the fish they ate on Friday should come from the sea, not from lake or river: if they had to buy frozen freshwater fish at the supermarket that day, they salted it heavily—another indication that salt was sex magic, "Friday" in Italian being *venerdì*, "Venus day." And did Nat know that some of the married women, but never the unmarried, wore good-luck amulets of rock salt around their necks, not removing them for years at a time? "Salt also implies good sense. A baby's lips are touched with salt during baptism; and because salt was formerly taboo on Sunday, there exists an Italian phrase *battezzato in domenica*—'baptized on Sunday'—meaning that a person is a fool."

When Nat contributed his memory of reading in a book by Ivan Morris that if Japanese nineteenth-century jingoists so much as glimpsed someone dressed in Western clothes they purified themselves by scattering salt, and that Jerzy Kosinski wondered in one of his stories why salt should be so expensive since God could make sinners into salt-pillars at will, he found that he had lowered his voice, like a conspirator.

Lyle did the same. "Always a touch of the sacred. You can see that customs couldn't help but be shocked when my friend spilled his salt on the ground. They probably thought of it as the seed of Onan."

Contrary to one of the superstitions, a grain of salt seemed in fact to have very little in common with a grain of common sense. And Nat was aware of feeling, as he never had before, that salt could be dangerous.

As THEY SAT over their wine, a white skiff glided into the Cala from behind one of the cliffs that projected from both sides like the wings of a watery stage. Only a very small craft was likely to come into that confined space under canvas: usually the rock faces would give back the sound of a motor. Skillfully guided, the sail approached the shore, then tacked and moved off.

"That's a trim sixteen-footer," Lyle remarked, absently; and then he gave a start and peered toward it, narrowing his eyes. "Or is it twelve?"

"Sixteen, I think."

"When Julia was married to Dick Goodspeed she used to say her life was a slow pickling in salt water, the twelve-footer he loved so was always awash. Now that she strolls the decks of a veritable *Queen Mary* you'd think she'd have no more such trouble. But I'm told that ancient though he is, L.K. has his own favorite twelve-footer, and that it's always on the *Nessie,* ready for instant use. I thought for a moment it might be him and Julia down there now. The *Nessie's* due here any day. This is the side of the island where you'd first catch sight of her."

"The Kaloumians actually carry a sailing boat on board their yacht? That seems scarcely possible—even a twelve-footer. It would have to be disassembled. And it would dry out, and . . ."

"I'm sure a skiff—plastic, no doubt—can be kept as wet and happy as any other passenger when you have acres of deck and a crew of dozens. Have you ever seen the *Nessie?* They say her so-called dinghy itself is the size of a railroad car. She's coming here via Palermo and Naples. If she's on schedule, my dear cousin is emptying the Naples boutiques this very minute. She's still into the shopping, they say."

In real life, a disclosure of Julia's huge dressmakers' bills had for a moment threatened to compromise her husband's career; and Lyle's portrayal of his heroine as having been driven by her unhappy childhood—deprived of the father she worshiped—into an almost insane compulsion to buy, especially to buy clothes, had been one of the book's more "compassionate" details.

Lyle himself had never entered politics; but in his novel, the statesman's wife encouraged her husband to sabotage the campaign of one of his own party's congressional candidates, to whom he was related, because of certain personal traits that might embarrass a potential aspirant to the presidency. The ostensible motive was conjugal devotion; the real, concern for herself alone, as possible future First Lady. The book's sharpest passages, following the details of the plane crash and the fictional widow's much publicized bereavement, mocked the disenchantment of the public when, casting off the national adulation, she married the billionaire twice her age whose unlovely face had for years illustrated newspaper stories of commercial and marital litigation. Cheated of the vision of the White House, Lyle's adventuress saw its only equivalent, the single other condition worthy of her precious self, in the celebrity of immeasurable wealth. Nor, in the novel, was her new life—on the surface so different from the old—any real change. The public had associated her with the social idealism which her husband had professed—but Lyle underlined "professed"; what the gullible public had swallowed was depicted by Lyle as the expertly concocted public image of a ruthless pair.

"Poor woman!" In real life that phrase, much used about the statesman's widow, was seldom heard about the plutocrat's wife. Especially after the publication of Lyle's book. (Though there were a perverse few who now applied the phrase to her precisely in her role as Lyle's victim.) As Mrs. Laurence Kaloumian, Julia had at first been photographed as much as before, and courted, though differently, perhaps even more. But during recent years facts had come to light that tended to dim her first husband's radiant reputation and bring both him and her closer to Lyle's fictitious figures.

Lyle had made his billionaire a caricature, even uglier than Julia's L.K. and more flamboyantly squalid. These days, L.K. appeared less frequently in the news, seemingly content to let his celebrated new wife run the show. His chief ostentation, apart from Julia herself, remained his floating palace, and even this he had given largely into Julia's charge. It had originally borne another name, the Christian name of an earlier Mrs. Kaloumian, a brawny Scot; and although its rebaptism by Julia was ostensibly an allusion to the vessel's own monstrous size and appearance, Julia was said to have remarked that it would have been ungracious to banish *all* reference to her predecessor. Julia often cruised in the *Nessie* with parties of guests, L.K. flying to join her from time to time, usually bringing with him contingents from one or more of his companies. Both Kaloumians were accustomed to the presence of armed guards, and the *Nessie*'s crew included a number of them. The yacht had the reputation of bringing an air of power, brutally protected power, to its ports of call.

Remembering Sacca's words about the island's peace, peculiar though certain aspects of that peace might be, Nat found the prospect of the *Nessie*'s arrival unpalatable. "Why is Julia coming here, Lyle?"

"Simply because she's never been, I suppose. I prophesy she won't stay long when she discovers the local shopping Sahara. And it's not a place I can imagine the King leaving his counting house for, either: he likes night life when he's on vacation. What will she do here? She'll have friends with her, but even so she'll have time on her hands."

"I suppose she will."

The phrase "living sequel" now took on more precise meaning. To visit, on the pretense of "research," a small island where one was almost certain to run into—by accident—one's estranged, and bored, cousin . . . Who knew what the confrontation might bring? Reconciliation? If so, wide press coverage, with photographs. Denunciation? An article or television appearance by Lyle, charged with sorrow about the continued misunderstanding and with perhaps a reference to the disenchanted mothers and liberals of America. Did it matter much what the result might be, as long as it was news?

"My God!" Lyle was suddenly shouting. "She's heading *toward* Naples!"

Far out, toward the mainland, there was moving a gray shape that seemed, in size, to be a small ocean liner, a slight reduction of an old second-string Cunarder. But only in size. Even from that distance the lines of this vessel could be seen as harshly contemporary—an angular hull, flat open decks fore and aft of a terraced bridge-and-cabin block, a single minimal funnel flanked by communications pylons like spiky obelisks. The hum of motors came over the water.

"Her schedule's off! She was supposed to leave Palermo yesterday! She must have waited till this morning!" The *Nessie's* change of schedule had put Lyle into near-frenzy. Even as he spoke, the ship passed out of sight, hidden by one of the Cala's cliffs.

Lyle was on his feet, shedding his caftan. "I'm going to run up to the village and see if she really crosses the bay. The whole town will be watching. Somebody will have binoculars. Take care of the check, will you? We'll straighten it out later." He disappeared into his bathhouse. When he emerged, in smart summer sports clothes, he waved and hurried off. At a distance he paused, turned, and called: "By the way, sorry to hear about your wife."

"Thank you."

"I daresay you'll get over it."

"I daresay."

Nat watched him take at a run the first few yards of the path toward his sequel. He was trim, but he'd have to slow down before long. And the smart clothes ... Unless one waited until well after siesta time, when the cliff-face fell into shadow, the shower one took following the climb from the Cala washed off more Mediterranean sweat than Mediterranean salt.

11

ALL WAS HOT and quiet at the Cala. No one else had come. The concessionaire was asleep in his deck chair. Nat took his book to a shady corner, but didn't turn many pages.

An hour or so later, in the water for a final dip before leaving, he retrieved thoughts that had surfaced as he began to doze, only to resubmerge in sleep. Melba had asked him, the other day, how he happened to be in noisy, unattractive Salerno; and now he wondered why she herself, though saying she longed for peace, had chosen to spend her one free day there. There were many quiet, pleasant places closer to Naples. Aspects of her disrepair haunted him: twenty-odd years had left disquieting marks.

When the sun went down he climbed back up the cliff to village level and made his way to the Imperatore. It was too early for Mario to have made his reappearance for the cocktail hour, and Nat walked unescorted through the lobby, onto the rear terrace, down the steps into the ruined garden. The flooded grass and plants were yellowed by hours of hot sun. He broke off stalks and leaves, smelled them, touched one or two with his tongue. A workman pushing a wheelbarrow called to him: "*Sale, sale—tutto sale!*"

It was what he had expected to taste.

THAT EVENING Immacolatina rang his bell. "Here's the salt I bought for you. The sample they let you have in Salerno will be gone before you know it." The new package was of good size, in an unlettered wrapping of bright indigo blue, quite unlike the usual printed containers proclaiming "Monopoli di Stato." When Nat reimbursed her—the price was higher than usual—she said: "It's for a good cause."

The "good cause" of the striking monopoly refiners? But provisioning with black-market salt, which he supposed this must be, could only harm that cause, could it not? Surely the strikers stood a better chance of winning if the country were salt-starved. Since there appeared to be no relation between salt and sense, was it possible that the strikers, in some convoluted strategy, were peddling black-market salt themselves?

"What is the good cause, Immacolatina?"

But the old lady's only reply, before bidding him good night, was the same illegible gesture from the regional repertory that she had made the night before.

12

ON SUNDAY Nat was wakened before seven by cacophony. After a moment he recognized and cursed it: throughout the week he managed to forget that earliest Sunday Mass on the island was inexorably proclaimed by a vocal rendering, broadcast through high-powered loudspeakers on the church roof, with carillon accompaniment, of an American song of the twenties:

> *There's a somebody I'm longing to see:*
> *I hope that He*

Turns out to be
Someone who'll watch over me,
Someone who'll watch over me . . .

Following his first Sunday's surprise, he learned that the local parish priest, the Parroco, had recently decided to supplement the old church bells by spending parish funds on an amplifying system and a series of cassettes. The priest had made his selection from an American catalogue, presumably by title, taking those which, as translated for him, struck him as religious. Nat brewed his coffee; and an hour later heard the second Mass announced, as usual, by the voice of the Church proclaiming its modernity:

Times they are a'changin' . . .

And he knew that noon High Mass, in this month of May dedicated to the Madonna, would bring:

For it is Mary, Mary, plain as any name can be . . .

followed in its turn by:

I've grown accustomed to her face . . .

During recent weeks, in fact, those two latter songs had been erupting each day, at any hour. The carillon never failed to drive Sacca into tirades, and this particular morning Nat heard him fulminating below to Immacolatina about "that Communist imbecile in the rectory."

The fifth and final number, always played as worshippers left the church at the close of the noon Mass, had become a noted feature of island life, and Nat had formed the habit of enjoying it, or rather its reception, on the terrace of a café in the piazza. Today as usual quite a few islanders and visitors had gathered there. The café tables were close beside the church, the amplifiers on its roof just above. A general air of expectancy could be sensed, increasing as the hands of the piazza clock approached twelve forty-five. Then there was a tremendous clang as the old bells were given brief throat, the doors of the church were thrown open, and the congregation began to stream out to an overwhelming, relentless pulsing of vocal and instrumental rock.

An American at the next table shouted to Nat through the din. "I've been told about this, but it's hard to believe. Have you seen the show the song's from?"

Nat hadn't.

"It's only X-rated, not porn, but still . . ."

"It's the title that counts."

Laughter had sprung up on all sides: it hadn't taken many weeks for both islanders and visitors to learn about the Deity's raucous demand that his people be allowed to "come." There was laughter both open and sniggering; laughter accompanied by looks of incredulity; or expressing, along with shrugs, recognition of the fact that these days, anything, anything at all, might be expected. Italian gestures being what they are, one could see the title being given in uninhibited translation to the uninitiated.

"*What was that?*" Nat asked the question of his neighbor; but his neighbor was all attention to the song. The detonation had been so very faint under the cover of the rock music that it had almost seemed to be extra percussion; but then it was repeated, and Nat knew it came from elsewhere. There were others who noticed it, as one could tell from a few looks that were exchanged, but no one paid further heed, so dominant was the Deity's yelling and thumping. And no sooner did the music stop than the crowd began to disperse, looking pleased, like an audience leaving a popular play.

Nat left too. If the blasts had been what they sounded like, he supposed the island grapevine would soon be carrying the news.

BUT THE NEWS that came was brought by a policeman.

The Carabiniere who rang his doorbell in mid-afternoon was brief, but had plainly been trained to use politeness with foreigners: visitors being among the island's chief sources of revenue, only those found to be penniless were treated with disrespect. He asked Nat whether he knew a Signor Brennan.

"Yes. Why? Has he been hurt?"

"Hurt? No, Professore, no!" The answer was emphatic: it took Nat a moment to realize that his question had seemed to suggest official manhandling. "Signor Brennan is simply hoping to see you."

"He is? Where?"

"At the Commissariato."

"I'll come at once."

On the way down it seemed preferable not to put questions about Lyle, but Nat asked whether the sounds heard at mid-day had indeed been explosions. The answer was short: "Albergo New-York."

"What happened?"

"Swimming pool."

The Albergo New-York was a holiday factory in a remote corner of the island, catering to package-tour groups and providing built-in entertainment—nightclub, bridge tournaments, sauna. The policeman was reluctant to give details of the incident, but piecemeal Nat learned a little. As at the Imperatore, no one had been injured. Sunday noon at the New-York was sacred to cookout, with the pool roped off against swimmers because the leading personality on the hotel's staff, a singing lifeguard celebrated in the tourist trade, led the guests, all joining in song behind him, to the barbecue pit in another part of the grounds, where he donned toque and apron and became singing chef.

"Any suspects?"

But that foolish question brought only silence.

At the police station a colleague of Nat's guide was sitting in a hallway outside a closed door marked "Commissario." He unlocked it, and there in a comfortably furnished office was Lyle, elegant as always, lounging in an overstuffed chair drinking an espresso. On the table was a tray. "If I'd thought sooner I'd have asked you to join me for lunch" was his greeting. "They do one rather well here—at one's own expense, of course. The risotto pescatore was particularly tasty. They had it sent in from the Fontana, which as you probably know is the only restaurant on this highly moralistic island rating a star in the Italian *Guide Michelin*."

The adjective told all.

"So you've been at it again, Lyle." So consistently had Lyle publicized this aspect of his life in his "Confessions" that there could be no question of impertinence.

Lyle shrugged. "The usual hypocrisy. And talk about discrimination! Look at me here in this luxury, and the poor wee bairn locked up down the street in a common cell. I was just out taking a walk to get as far away as I could from that ghastly music, and he happened along, like a gift from the gods."

"How wee is he?"

"Not too. Certainly over the age of consent. It's not age that's making the difficulty. It seems our being on a public road could technically make it a public scandal. But who expects the police to come charging down a leafy byway? And even so, wouldn't you think they'd keep their minds on their work—in this particular case the explosions they were on their way to investigate? But no: they had to stop and put what's known as the worst possible construction on our being there. Actually there'd been no time for anything to happen, though I don't deny I was hoping for the best. It could have been idyllic."

Preoccupied by the New-York affair, the Commissario had ordered Lyle held until he could interview him. "Nothing new in being held, need I say. In the old days we were always in and out of police stations, few of them as comfortable as this." The Commissario would probably be arriving soon. Lyle apologized to Nat for bringing him out, but he felt he had to show the authorities that he had a friend among the island's "respectable element." "And that's you, Herr Doktor." One of the policemen had taken down vital statistics: by now he had doubtless telephoned to Venice and had it confirmed that Lyle himself was officially respectable in that region, a tax-paying foreign resident in good standing. "That being the case, I think the people here will simply ask me to leave the island. But I don't want to leave just yet."

"You'd miss your living sequel."

Lyle didn't deny it. "Maybe they'll let me stay since I know such an eminent Psychographer."

"Have you told them you're a cousin of you know who?"

" 'The Catholic Laywoman of the Year'?" (Julia, prominent in Catholic affairs, had in the past received various Church awards.) "Good God no. If she got wind of this she'd beg them to lock me up for life."

After a time voices and movement could be heard, the door was unlocked, and the portly Police Chief, last seen by Nat the day before near the Imperatore, entered his office with a party of henchmen. He and Nat were acquainted only ex-officio—it was his office that granted residence permits—and his brusque, inattentive greeting made it clear that in the present crisis these two foreigners were too unimportant to expect attention. "Oh, yes. Please stay on the island," he said, when one of the others reminded him who Lyle was. "We may want your testimony in a larger matter." He gave Nat a second look, as though appointing him Lyle's bondsman. Then he nodded toward the door and an aide opened it.

The hall was crowded: Nat recognized the detectives from Rome and most of the island's police force. Lyle was not put off by numbers or by the atmosphere of emergency. "May I have a word with the boy?" he coolly asked the officer who had opened the door. "I know where he is." A nod; and Nat's earlier guide accompanied them out of the building.

The courthouse was a few hundred yards up the street, and unlike the Commissario's office its basement was bare and smelled strongly of disinfectant. Inside a barred enclosure a guard, sitting at a table, looked up from his newspaper. A few words in dialect and the gate was unlocked. Nat waited outside. Within, Lyle was asked to remove his jacket, frisked, and motioned to approach the cells.

These stretched in a short row beyond an intervening space. Far back in one of them stood a slight, fair-haired young man, who did not move forward as Lyle approached, and whose features, though indistinct, gave Nat a sense of déjà vu. Only one other cell was occupied: in it someone was lying motionless on a cot, perhaps asleep.

At the table a conversation in dialect was taking place between guard and guide. Nat could follow parts of it.

"As we led him in here past Giacomo, Giacomo greeted him, but the young one wouldn't even look at him."

"Why should he? Giacomo told on him."

"Giacomo had to. For Giacomo the alibi was essential. Does anybody know who the boy is?"

"Not yet. His papers are false."

"Will he be investigated?"

"Who knows?"

"You mean it depends?"

"Doesn't it always?"

Later, while Lyle was putting on his jacket, the guard addressed him as "Signor Conte." (Islanders, sometimes in hope of reward, though often simply in tribute to a show of personal style, would confer complimentary titles on foreigners.) "If the Signor Conte is interested in the Signorino, he could in full confidence leave something with me that would ensure an improvement in his nourishment."

Lyle counted out some notes from his wallet. "An appropriate percentage of this for you, of course. And"—with a glance at the guide—"no doubt for you too? Take care of him."

Thanks were drowned out by the clanging of keys and gate.

They walked back to the piazza.

"I wonder if I haven't seen your young friend somewhere before."

"Perhaps. I'd seen him myself, at the Imperatore, where I'm staying. He works—or worked until today—in the bar pantry there."

"Then he's the one that got the watchman drunk."

Lyle hadn't heard about that. "So he's inside because of being close to two bombings, whereas I just now offered to pay for a lawyer, thinking it was because of his being close to me. How conceited can one get? There's no question of the lawyer, by the way. The boy didn't even answer my offer. Wouldn't speak a word to me, as a matter of fact. Too bad. I was nourishing dreams of a beautiful friendship."

Lyle's regret at the refusal of his offer—scarcely altruistic—to "pay for a lawyer" might represent more than mere disappointment at the dashing of erotic hopes. The element of the two bombings, reinforcing the otherwise innocuous episode of the roadway meeting, might, on further acquaintance with the boy, have provided material for a future "Confession." In fact Nat thought he remembered the line "He happened along, like a gift from the gods" as already having been used in one of the television installments. Temporary banishment from the island was the usual penalty imposed on foreigners charged with sexual offenses. In the past, such peccadillos had often been ignored; but modern mores being what they are, the tourist bureau was concerned lest the island's pagan reputation for aphrodisia get wildly out of hand. In any case, Lyle had nothing to fear from interrogation about the Albergo New-York explosions: he had simply happened to be walking in the vicinity. It was the boy who would have explaining to do. Nat, not himself involved, felt inexplicably disturbed by the affair.

"Au revoir, Herr Parole-Offizier," Lyle said, as they separated in the piazza. "By the way, I wonder whether my sylvan eroticism played tricks with my hearing this morning. Tell me: what was that last number broadcast from the church? It couldn't have been . . ."

"It was, though."

"What a headline! 'Writer Jailed for Attempting to Obey Injunction of Almighty'!"

The episode might, after all, find its way to the home screen.

Nat had almost reached his flat when he thought of something and turned back.

13

WHAT HE DID was to stop in at the Imperatore and ask the concierge whether the Albergo New-York pool used salt water. The answer was yes. It and the Imperatore's had been the only salt-water pools on the island until the recent opening of a third, at a new establishment called Swank. Did the Professore know Swank, perhaps? The Professore had heard of it; and the concierge agreed with his observation that its proprietors might be feeling nervous just now. "Though I don't see what they can do by way of prevention except keep watch," he said. "So far as I know, neither we nor the New-York was sent any kind of ultimatum. Each seems like a case of sheer vandalism."

That evening, and throughout the night, Nat tried to arrange the bombings, the refiners' strike, blue-packaged salt, and Immac-olatina's "It's all in a good cause" into some kind of pattern. None emerged; and he desisted, reminding himself that in crime stories even a professional sleuth is seldom able to formulate a theory until after a third incident. Would the newcomer, Swank, have to blow up before an explanation was forthcoming? He speculated about this traditional requirement of three for a solution. Perhaps inspired by the classicism of his present surroundings, he thought of the Priestess's tripod at Delphi. No tripod, no oracle. The present affair was only two-legged so far. Too tottery to support a theory.

OLD PRIESTESSES came to mind again in the morning, while the funicular connecting village and harbor was taking him down on his usual Monday quest for weekend newspapers at the kiosk on the quay. One compartment of the car was packed with nuns. In Italy, where churches bring to mind the pagan temples on whose foundations or within whose ruins they were often built, and priests' vestments and monks' robes recall the toga, the flocks of nuns are vestal virgins, priestesses as of old. The nuns of the order which had its convent on the island had made no concession to modern change in dress. The hems of their skirts trailed in the dust, they were as amply veiled and stiffly coiffed as always. It was unusual to see more than one or a pair of them at a time, but there must have been ten or twelve in the funicular. When the car emptied at harbor level Nat saw them cross the quay toward the pier.

The newspapers had arrived by early morning hydrofoil—the London *Times, Sunday Times* and *Observer;* and the *International Herald-Tribune* and *Daily American.* He bought them all and sat down at a café on the quayside. A series of whistle blasts was announcing the imminent departure of a steamer; an agitation of black veils before a ticket window transformed itself into a black slipstream along the pier as the vestals ran for it. Someone chuckled beside Nat's chair. It was Sacca.

"Off to Sorrento! Good luck, girls!"

"What is it, an excursion?"

"An excursion with a purpose!"

After momentary hesitation, Sacca consented to join him. Relations between landlord and tenant had always been discreet; this was the first example of what could be called socializing. "They're off to see the Archbishop. And not just to kiss his ring, either."

Nat looked his question, and Sacca answered with one of his own: "What do you think of the carillon?"

Nat laughed, and Sacca caught his meaning and was instantly in full cry of agreement, the objects of his blast this morning being less the Parroco and his loudspeakers than those of the islanders who remained indifferent or who even liked "that trash." "They're trash themselves! Cretini! Gentaglia! Barbari!" Sacca was well known locally in his role of castigator; his voice was not low; passersby along the quay registered by grin or nod their recognition of what was taking place.

"Visitors to the island find us old inhabitants simple people, and perhaps we are simple, Professore. But we have our tastes, and we can be outraged." The "really respectable old families" were up in arms. They had all written to the Archbishop at Sorrento, the Parroco's immediate superior. "You should do the same, Professore! Indignation is not enough! Write to the Archbishop!"

"I will. Gladly. Though as a foreigner . . ."

"No, no! Foreign voices speak louder than ours. Write, Professore!"

"I will, I will. So those nuns . . ."

"They're doing more than writing. You know their convent, beside the church. The carillon drives them mad. Mad! Especially because the Parroco bought it with their money. Since he came last year he has refused to pay the convent its share of the offerings taken in the church—a tradition of centuries. The convent has always been considered part of the church, Professore. You know it occupies . . ."

Nat knew the convent, on the edge of the island's casbah—or rather one of its two casbahs. The medieval village, high above the harbor, successor to the acropolis of the ancient Greek settlement, had consisted of two separate rabbit warrens, one on each side of the present piazza—twin mazes of alleys, courts and culs-de-sac, most of them now whitewashed, and some tunneled under fortress-like dwellings and lit by streetlamps at all hours. In the old days they were the fiefs of rival factions, often in bloody conflict. The former occupants of the building now housing the nuns had left during one of the periodic expulsions of monastic orders, and the cells and other rooms had been let out as lodgings. Later, under the 1929 Concordat, part of it had been restored and allotted to the sisters.

"You mean the monks always shared in the offerings, and the nuns resumed the sharing when they came, but this Parroco says they're not entitled?"

"Exactly. And with the money that should go to them he buys the carillon."

"So the nuns . . ."

"The Archbishop didn't answer Fedora's letter. And you know Fedora."

"I don't, though."

"Madre Serafina. The Mother Superior. Fedora in the family—she was a Sacca, a cousin. You must have seen her in the village. She doesn't go unnoticed."

"You mean that tall, *striding* nun?"

"Exactly. Tall. And as you say: striding. She waited two weeks for the Archbishop to answer. Yesterday she telephoned to Sorrento, not letting on who she was, to make sure he'd be there today. They'll be reaching Sorrento in a few minutes." Sacca smiled. "If you knew Fedora . . ."

"I begin to feel I do."

"A dozen round trips to Sorrento is no small item, especially when your parish priest has slashed your funds. They couldn't be doing it without help."

"Contributions were made?"

"By many. Including yourself."

"By me?"

Sacca nodded.

"In what form?"

Sacca's forefinger was beside his nose, in another of those gestures eloquent enough if one has the key. "Come, Professore, I don't think I've set you much of a riddle. Just think, and you'll find the answer in a second. When you do, please don't share it. It's an island secret—by which I mean that most of the island knows, but doesn't talk. Arrivederci! Grazie del caffè! Arrivederci!"

In his politely abrupt way he rose, shook hands, and left. Nat saw him enter the funicular station, homeward bound.

So the convent had benefited from the purchase of blue-packaged salt? Everything touched on these days seemed to turn saline. Forgotten tags swarmed up. *Many fresh streams meet in one salt sea. Let your speech always be seasoned with salt* could be the slogan of whoever sought a solution. "Solution!" Even that had its salty sound. What was Madre Serafina's role in the anti-monopoly, if it was anti-monopoly? He didn't suppose she set bombs, though Sacca had made her sound capable of almost anything. Where was the third leg of the tripod?

He returned to his newspapers.

The *American* carried a story about the *Nessie*, with pictures. Mrs. Kaloumian had left the yacht at Naples and flown to Rome "for a few days' shopping." That was logical enough: Rome had the dressmakers—and so much more. "When she returns south Mr. Kaloumian is expected to join her for a cruise among the islands."

Lyle would be impatient.

DINING ALONE on his terrace that evening, he heard Sacca's telephone ring; and shortly thereafter came the familiar sounds of a tantrum. Plainly a major one, for he heard Immacolatina cry: "Calm yourself! Calm yourself!" But the volume increased as Sacca emerged onto his own terrace, just below. He was sufficiently beside himself to abandon landlordly discretion. Seeing Nat, he shouted up. Out of his distorted face came a war cry: *"Guerra! Guerra!"*

"Calm yourself!"

"The Archbishop's a ———! A ———! A ——— with a swollen ———! A———!"

"Shame! People in the street! Calm yourself, for God's sake!"

"The Archbishop's a ———! And the Parroco's his bastard!"

Nat cried *"What!,"* forgetting that, in Italian invective as practiced by an artist, hyperbole is one of a painter's bright tones.

"Can it be otherwise? Can His Excellency really approve that electronic barrel organ? No! Can His Excellency really approve the embezzlement of funds? No! But he pretends to. Why? To protect his idiot son, and to protect himself lest the bastard talk. What do we know of this parroco? Who ever heard of him before he came? Out of the Archbishop's ——— one night or siesta-time. Nine months inside some ———'s ———. Then kept a secret, and now brought out to be the penance of us all!"

Immacolatina was stifling laughter with her apron. Sacca sat down, wiping his face. The storm abruptly subsided. "Well," he said, in a different voice, "there must be some such explanation, mustn't there?"

"The excursion to Sorrento was fruitless?"

"Fruitless? Nothing Fedora does is fruitless. The fruit will be a different kind, that's all. Bitterer—for those pimps. Pimps! Bastards!" Rage, reviving, brought new invective. "Eunuchi! Ruffiani!"

Immacolatina moaned and fled inside.

Calm returned. The Archbishop's reply to the nuns, it

seemed, had been that the matters they brought to his attention were of purely local concern, up to the Parroco's discretion. The Archbishop himself washed his hands of them. And Sacca said with solemnity: "I can only reiterate, Professore, that this island is now at war. *War.* It has been declared. Formally. Formally," he repeated, as he re-entered his flat. "Formally declared. Mark my word."

AFTER DINNER Nat took a walk. Few people were about; on the belvedere beyond the piazza the air was soft. Naples glowed across black miles of bay; the towns to the south were an arc of lights. Down the steps from the church came toward him a small man in black, with a white English setter following. He was youngish, looked thoughtful, a little pinched, wore glasses and a clerical collar. As he and Nat passed in the empty piazza they exchanged salutations. Nat couldn't recall having seen him before. Was it only at night that he dared come out? He called his dog. For an instant, Nat considered the possibility that he himself was obsessed. But no: through the darkness the call was repeated. "Sally!" the priest called. "Sally, vieni!"

Sale!

In the night the loudspeakers on the church roof were dimly visible. From the monastery-convent next door, though its windows were closed and dark, there came—he had noticed it before when passing the spot—an aroma of coffee. He entered the old quarter, all alleys and tunnels, steps and ramps between high walls, few streetlamps, blind corners. "What a place for street fighting!" The words, spoken to himself, were the only reminder that the island was now a war zone.

14

THE MORNING'S MAIL brought Nat a clipping from a Great Lakes newspaper, sent by a friend at home—"Thought you'd be interested." Its illustration was a photograph of a painting he knew well, captioned "Rumored Sold to Trustee."

The article concerned a court injunction being sought by the children of a couple who had bequeathed a group of paintings to the Art Gallery housing the Deming collection. According to the plaintiffs, when the university accepted the bequest—after, indeed, having solicited it—it had agreed to "permanently retain" the pictures; whereas "a number have recently been sold to individual trustees and art dealers, and others are scheduled to be disposed of by auction." The children, "motivated by respect for their parents' memory," were asking the court to prohibit the university from further dispersing the collection.

A telephone inquiry yesterday to one of the trustees, who asked not to be named, brought the response that Mr. and Mrs. Levean had merely "requested" that the pictures be retained, and that the university had duly "acknowledged the request" but did not feel legally bound to respect it. Asked whether it was the practice of the university to sell paintings from its collection, the trustee replied that sales were made "occasionally."

Asked further concerning rumors that recent sales have included several paintings from the Jason Deming collection of Italian masters, the trustee refused to confirm or deny the reports. "Like any other owner," he said, "the university can of course dispose of its possessions as it sees fit. The de-accessioning of a picture and the use of the proceeds would simply represent a redistribution of the university's assets. It can be stated categorically that any picture de-accessioned from the university's collection would have been deemed by qualified members of the art department to be non-relevant to current taste."

Recent visitors to the university's art gallery have reported that a number of the Deming pictures are missing from their usual places on the walls, and there has been speculation concerning an auction sale scheduled to be held in New York later this year and billed as including pictures from "a Midwestern Educational Institution."

"Non-relevant to current taste"!

A century earlier, it was because American dealers and members of several art departments had scorned the Deming pictures as non-relevant to then current taste that the Midwestern Educational Institution had been able to get them for so little. Now the Institution was "de-accessioning" for the same reason. What would its art department buy instead? It was possible to imagine a postscript to that newspaper story, perhaps a statement by one of the department's "qualified members":

Funds accruing from the de-accessioning of redundant paint-ings are generally put toward the acquisition of objects of a kind now more than formerly admitted to the canon of Fine Art. "Found Objects" are one such category. For example, a particularly beautifully weathered telephone pole was re-cently installed in the art gallery's Great Hall. We are gradually strengthening our collection of superb examples of American plumbing fixtures from the early years of the present century. Attendance records show that such exhibits attract large numbers of visitors. It is always our aim to enhance our usefulness to the public.

Who would have the last laugh? If buyers for "redundant" Deming pictures were currently to be found among dealers and the trustees themselves . . . Dealers have sharp eyes for discards. And whenever did a trustee buy a picture for his own private collection without consulting a dealer? The "qualified members" might be likened, in their complacency, to the Parroco, who was sure that the cassettes of his choice were broadcasting the word of God.

In the piazza he encountered Lyle, who said he had heard nothing from the police. "My angelo is still in the lockup, I take it?"

"Is Angelo his name? Or is the *a* small?"

"It's how I think of him, alas."

Lyle was carrying a beach bag, and saw Nat's. "The Cala as before?"

"I thought of taking a look at Swank."

"Mind if I join you?"

"Come along."

Lyle was plainly at loose ends. He had seen the small item in the *American*. "Julia's shopping will be the death of me. If anybody but you were my bail bond I think I'd skip to Rome and hope for something to happen there."

Swank, a newly opened bathing and restaurant establishment, which boasted the island's third salt-water pool, was out on one of the farther promontories. Its owners were not locals, and their posters in several languages publicized the remote situation, which made arrival by land difficult, as offering particular amenity to those "fortunate enough to possess their own craft and desiring an atmosphere of exclusive tranquillity." Smaller print offered ferry service from the marina for those less blessed. The snob appeal caused amusement among the islanders, for there were few households so unfortunate as not to possess, or to have cousins who possessed, "their own craft," if only in the form of a battered rowboat with or without motor.

Nevertheless, as Nat and Lyle approached their destination in Swank's ferry—a sleek speedboat whose helmsman's T-shirt was emblazoned with the establishment's name and which rushed them on their way as though they were emergency patients in a water ambulance—they saw that a number of the fortunate had responded to the posted advertisements. The island often had more nautical visitors than one was aware of from the village; today quite a flotilla was at anchor in Swank's indentation of the rocky shore. Among those craft, and past a few swimmers who preferred the sea to the pool above, the ferry approached the landing stage. A small motor yacht had just debarked its passengers and was moving off. Nat saw the name on its stern, and looked upward: nearing the top of Swank's stairs were the Salerno-Paestum heroes and girls. By the time the ferry was alongside they had disappeared from view.

But not from earshot. Shouting came from above.

"Whaddya mean, search?"

"Don't you dare touch my bag!"

"Oh, Madame . . ."

"Listen, Buster . . ."

"Please, Harry, not a fight!"

"What kind of a place is this?"

"Sir, let me explain . . ."

"Well well! *Here's* a surprise!" By the time Lyle said that, he and Nat had climbed the stairs and reached the entrance gate, where the heroes and girls were glaring at a blond youth wearing Swank's T-shirt. He was failing utterly to pacify them, and someone heavier and darker was hurrying toward the gate from inside, with a grim air of providing reinforcement.

The boy was speaking an English that was part British, part American, with Italian overtones, and occasionally hesitant. "It is for your own safety, ladies and gentlemen. We are . . . requesting that you allow us to . . . inspect your bags in case someone has . . . tricked you and . . . inserted . . ."

Nat was puzzled. Seen clearly, the young face was certainly reminiscent, as it had been even in the cell, of some face he knew; and today the intonations, too, were familiar.

"Of all the goddam impositions. . . . Jesus, look who's here!"

The American sextet drowned Nat in a crescendo of greeting.

The boy had moved off without giving Lyle a sign of recognition, and the heavy from within was trying to take over, adding to the din his Neapolitan-American pleas for reasonableness. Harry the choker: "So what if nobody else objected? Bet none of those nobodies were 'murricans."

Eventually, with beach bags patted rather than inspected, all the new arrivals were inside, clustered at the counter to pay Swank's entrance fee. Learning that the sextet had only that morning stepped onto the island, Nat offered them a few words of enlightenment concerning the reasons for precaution, and they dispersed amicably enough to bathhouses, promising "See you at the pool."

Swank's manager, drawn out of his office by the fracas, responded to what he heard Nat say. Yes, inspection had been instituted the day before. Unfortunately, the heavy's slightly crude performance of his duties had offended a few sensibilities, and he was now kept inside, reserved for "special cases." Just this morning he had been replaced at the gate by the young man they had seen. *His* correctness must have impressed them, no? He was so well brought up. Educatissimo. "The son of a principessa. A student at the University of Naples."

"Then might one ask," Lyle said, "why he isn't in class?"

"Because, Signore, the university is closed."

Nat knew from the newspapers that it was open. What could be going on? This single suspect, known to have been close to the scene of both explosions, jailed, his papers false, was now sprung and taken on as a watchdog against a possible new explosion.

"Is the jail your hiring hall?" Lyle lit a cigarette.

"Jail, Signore? I don't understand. The young man presented himself for employment just when he was needed. We're lucky to have him."

Lyle strolled a few yards to the gate. The boy was there again, looking out to sea, awaiting arrivals. He had certainly overheard. "Is the charge against you dropped, then?"

"Charge? What charge, Sir?" He gazed at Lyle without expression. The face was peculiarly pale, the features were fine, a little drawn; an ascetic face, Nat found it, in one so young.

Lyle persisted. "When did they let you out?"

"Out of where, Sir?"

Back at the counter, Lyle said: "I'll telephone, if I may."

"Alas, Signore, out of order."

The telephone chose that moment to ring: even the manager had to smile. He sobered quickly as he answered. "Yes, Signor Commissario, he came and is at work. No, Signor Commissario. Certainly, Signor Commissario . . ."

Lyle didn't wait for the end. "Come along, Nat. Let's swim if we're going to. My call's been made for me. I was going to ask whether our young friend has joined the local police force. The affirmative answer came. Really astonishingly bilingual, isn't he! I hadn't the slightest hint of it."

They moved off.

"You really think he's working for the police?" '

"You heard the manager. More precisely, working for Swank in cooperation with the police."

"But why should the police cooperate with *him?* Why let him out? You think he's turned informer?"

"Looks like it."

"And all of them—the police, Swank, and the boy—are working together against the bombers?"

"Can you think of a better explanation?"

Nat had none to offer: there was still no third leg for the tripod.

As THEY APPROACHED the poolside, the girl who had called from the afterdeck of the *Gattopardo II* in Salerno now repeated her invitation: "This time do join us for a tooni!"; and Nat, accepting, presented Lyle. Even the awe generated by the live presence of a television celebrity—"We wondered if it could really be you!"—delayed only minimally the inevitable detailed saga of the cemetery cruise. The unsatisfactory behavior of the skipper dominated the narrative. He had put the party through "a grueling week"; but he'd be taking them to Naples the next day, and that would be the end of him, thank God.

That very morning, on arriving at the island—"this is typical"—he had advised them to take a taxi and spend the day at the Albergo New-York, which according to him "had everything." But being by now savvy, they had checked at the tourist bureau on the quay and learned that the New-York's swimming pool was out of commission. "Needless to say, nobody told us why." Swank was recommended instead. " 'So, take the ferry to Swank,' Gatto said." Take the ferry, when they were paying for a yacht! He claimed the island's coastal waters were full of reefs, hazardous to navigation by non-natives. They checked on that, too: "old salts" at the harbor laughed—" 'What reefs?' " Gatto was furious. He was down there on the boat now, sulking because they'd told him to wait: he'd wanted to return to the marina—they could at least take the ferry back, couldn't they? "We're sick of his dodges. Remember he said there were no landing facilities at Paestum and we paid for taxis and let him spend the day in Salerno? We were still green then: we found out later we could perfectly well have landed in a small boat. Always some excuse to stay in port by himself and send us off for the day. He's a nut. Once we came back aboard earlier than expected and he raised holy hell. Accused us of spying on him.

More than once he had somebody in his cabin he wouldn't let us see—a woman, probably. He can have all the women he wants, but . . ."

"If you're so sick of him," Lyle interrupted, "why prolong the agony? Pay him off pronto and be free."

"We're already paid up in advance through tomorrow."

"Get your gear off his boat. Kiss him good-bye. Spend the night in a nice hotel on the island and take the hydrofoil to Naples in the morning on your own."

"Why should we pay for a hotel and a hydrofoil when we've already paid for everything inclusive?"

Lyle's undisguised groan was partially drowned by the voice of one of the girls. "If you want to see what the crumb looks like, there he is at the counter now."

They glanced that way. The Sicilian skipper of the *Gattopardo II* was placing a parcel wrapped in bright indigo blue on the counter of Swank's office, and pointing toward his boat.

A few minutes later the blond youth was seen, gliding among the poolside deck chairs and disappearing into Swank's bamboo-enclosed bar-restaurant at the far end, in whose inner dimness two barely discernible people were sitting. One of them got up and came out with the youth—a man now seen to have a beak of a nose, and conspicuous among the bathers and sunbathers for being in city clothes, complete even to hat. He tapped a sunbather, who rose and followed him. They passed the office, disappeared beyond the gate; before long they reappeared, without the youth. The city man re-entered the bar.

The sextet continued to discuss their "problem." Lyle, turning the pages of a magazine found on a nearby deck chair, looked up once to wag his head in their direction and mouth "Idiots!" to Nat.

Certain actions were making Nat nervous.

The sunbather who had been with the city man entered a bathhouse.

"I think Lyle's right," Nat said, abruptly. "Why not get your things off the boat now and let him go, before . . ."

"Before tomorrow morning?" They showed signs of taking umbrage at being advised yet again. "Maybe we're capable of making up our own minds," the tooni girl suggested.

Nat had not meant "before tomorrow morning."

The sunbather who had entered the bathhouse emerged carrying goggles, snorkel and spear. Once again he made his way toward the gate, this time alone.

"I'm for sticking it out," one of the Americans muttered. "Instead of handing the bastard twenty-four hours' pay on a platter."

"And getting insulted for our pains."

The "bastard" was still at the counter. His conversation with the manager seemed not to be entirely satisfactory. He made a move as though to leave, taking up the sample of his wares; but the manager gestured to him to wait, and picked up the telephone.

The call was a long one. It occurred to Nat that the manager might be keeping the cradle depressed.

The skin diver returned from the sea. Still dripping, his gear beside him, he stretched out again in his poolside chair in the sun.

After the manager finally hung up and said a few words, the "bastard" shrugged, took up his blue parcel, glanced toward the pool as though to see whether his employers were watching, and disappeared.

Nat stood up. "I'm for a dip in the sea."

He went as far as the parapet and looked down at the anchored craft. On the landing stage the skipper was about to board a small boat to take him out to the $^{\text{G A T T O P A R D O}}_{\text{P A L E R M O}}$ $^{\text{I I}}$. But . . . On the skipper's astonished face Nat read his discovery of what he himself had just that moment seen. What was happening to the *Gattopardo?* P A L E R M O had vanished entirely. And of the other letters on the stern, all that was visible above the waterline was $_{\text{G A T T O P A R D O}}$ $_{\text{I I}}$. Even as Nat watched, that too disappeared; and in moments, with shocking acceleration, the entire little yacht foundered, gurgling as it plunged, and leaving only a whirlpool of bobbing debris—deck cushions, a litter of light equipment, someone's lolly-pink plastic windbreaker.

The skipper's Sicilian roar brought people hurrying from deck chairs and out from the pool; within a few moments Nat was being pushed against the parapet by a mass of excited, curious humanity in bikinis and bathing trunks. He shouted in alarm; using all his force he managed to turn and ram, butt, shove his way out. Swank's manager was hurrying down to the landing stage; the pool's lifeguard was following after; barman and waiters had run out from the bar and joined the throng. Except for Nat, and for Lyle, who was standing apart, the space adjoining the pool and the bar-restaurant was empty. Nat was sweating, savoring his escape.

It was then that he saw Melba appear from within, framed in the doorway of the bar. It took him a moment to recognize her, she was so fashionably dressed. She looked distraught, and was pulling herself free from the man in city clothes behind her, who had a hand on her arm. "*Ladi!*" she called, quite stridently. "*Ladi!*" And as she caught sight of Nat it was almost a repetition of the encounter in Salerno, so little surprised did she seem that he too should be there. "Oh, have you seen Laddie?" she appealed, anglicizing the name. "Is Laddie all right, at least?"

From somewhere in the crowd, above the shouting there rose the shrill whistling of a musical phrase. As it was repeated, Melba smiled. She held out her hand to Nat with the easy grace learned at the Sacred Heart. "How very nice to see you again," she said, in her English that was like the English he had heard at the gate. "When things are quieter, we must sit down again somewhere for a little chat. Remember, I said I have things to tell you."

Out of the crowd the "angelo," Laddie, came straight up to them. If Melba's dove-gray hair hadn't been close in tone to the boy's blondness, the resemblance between them would have been less noticeable. Melba turned to Nat. "This is my nephew—" she began. But just then someone called "Principessa!"; and, as though recognizing urgency, she broke off and hurried away.

Over where he was standing alone, Lyle, at this same moment, cried "The *Nessie!*" and Nat saw that yacht's great gray shape looming on the sea.

PART TWO

15

THE NIGHT BEFORE the encounter with Nat in Salerno, Melba had been kept awake until well after twelve by the scampering and chewing in the sealed-off salotto and the throbbing of the jukebox overhead. Later, the jukebox roused her from sleep shortly before dawn. That was a rare occurrence: it very seldom resumed before late afternoon or evening, when members arrived at the Club and began to talk among themselves or on the telephone. Melba knew they played it to cover their voices. She knew also that a member would occasionally sleep in the Club room. She suspected that this time there had been an early hour telephone ring, unheard by her, which had triggered the resumption of the music.

The throbbing continued: probably other telephone conversations were being covered. Then she heard, from below, the clang of the wicket cut into one of the halves of the palazzo's great wooden street door. There was tramping on the stairs. Her doorbell rang. Wrapping herself in a dressing gown, she called out to the ringer to identify himself, then opened.

Signor Vispo apologized for the disturbance. (Formal address prevailed between them: on his return to Naples several years before, he had let her know, obliquely but unmistakably, that he would resume the old "Principessa" if she dropped the old "Pasquale.") As the Principessa could imagine, it was only a very special emergency that would force him to wake her. An unforeseen job had to be done out of town. Would she go? It was not a mission on which he would ordinarily send her. A man would be more suitable. But since it called for someone of class, someone who could not possibly be recognized as an emissary of the Committee—he explained that that was what the Club was henceforth to be called: the "Committee"—and since Don Ladislao was elsewhere . . .

The "Don" was another part of the unspoken pact. No one was better placed than Signor Vispo to know that Ladislao had no such title—Ladislao, who looked like Melba though there was no reason why he should. For one thing, since Italy had become a republic, titles no longer legally existed: to speak of them now was to speak of archaeology; everyone knew that. Nevertheless, they continued to be used. And despite the new family laws, the *Libro d'oro* continued to insist that only children who were both "natural" (that is, not adopted), and—archaic term!—"legitimate" had the right to any title whatever. Ladislao did not meet that requirement. In such a situation, sensitivity and respect (Melba preferred those terms to "bargaining") were what counted; and she took comfort in thinking that Signor Vispo had both. Along, admittedly, with other qualities.

"One of Ladì's professors telephoned me yesterday to ask where he was, why he wasn't back at the university after the Easter vacation. I was hard put to answer, not knowing myself where he is. How much longer will he be away?"

"Not more than a week, if all goes well."

"*If!* You guaranteed his safety."

"I did and I do. But I warned you a slight delay is always possible."

"Meanwhile his education suffers."

"Principessa . . ."

The tone was admonitory, reminding Melba of the truth: that without Club assignments there would be no university for Ladislao. "I hope and pray he'll not be expelled for truancy."

Signor Vispo smiled. "You think of your convent school, Principessa. If I had been fortunate enough to attend the university, no one could have called me truant had I stayed away. University students have always come and gone at will. It is part of the privileged life they lead. If Don Ladislao's professor telephoned, it was out of personal regard."

That was likely. All Laddie's professors admired him, and must have missed him. As for missing . . . What she herself foolishly missed, these days, were the bright opening bars of "Questa o quella" that Laddie always whistled up to her window on his return from class. (Melba connected his choice of song with the fact that quite often, when the telephone rang, it was a girl—not always the same one—asking for Laddie.)

"Principessa: time passes. Will you . . . ?"

There was no question of refusing. The bank account needed constant replenishing. The University Fund, she called it to herself. Impossible to know how much longer it would be essential. Laddie was approaching the end of his second year, the time for choosing his field. What would he aim at? Law? Medicine? Engineering? Commerce? Nowadays it would be thought shameful if a young man in Laddie's position wasn't allowed to train himself for a profession. There would be scholarships later, for such a student as he. Meanwhile, a heavy burden. And of late Laddie had shown a new, strange indisposition to talk of the future. Hints, questions, brought no answer. He was always affectionate, sweet-natured. But for some time now, inscrutable.

"This mission should appeal to you, Principessa. To your tender heart. A mission of humanity."

The instructions were clear. In its way, this was a simple assignment. Different, for example, from the complicated first one, which had taken her into places she had never expected to visit— government ministries in Rome. Finding the right office in each of the maze-like buildings, finding the right man in each office, delivering the right envelope to the right man: without (she had been told this was crucial) letting any one of them suspect she was seeing the others. That first job had resulted in the return to the Club room of several pallid members, following absences of a readily conjectured kind. Signor Vispo's praise included a reminder that hiring her had been his own excellent idea: "Well, Principessa, our—your—success is complete. It justifies my belief in the benefits of education. Such finesse! If I ever have a daughter, I think I will ask you to recommend her to your old teachers. It would be a sound investment."

Her old teachers! Long in their graves, ces Dames! Melba doubted that even today their successors would welcome to Trinità dei Monti the daughter of a Vispo. Indeed she was beginning to wonder whether Signor Vispo's increasingly frequent words about education might not contain a touch of—what? Irony? Surely she had done the best she could for him. Who would have done more? But his compliment had been accompanied by something there was no uncertainty about—a bonus; and there had been subsequent bonuses.

Would there be one for today?

16

In the morning bus, headed for Salerno, Melba let her fancy play on how things might have been.

Ordinarily she was too busy for daydreaming. Sitting at her courtyard window when not doing errands in Via Lupo or trudging up and down the palazzo staircases, she was available to all: to receive rents (but more often complaints), direct repairs, listen to tales, commiserate, congratulate, placate, scold. The Principessa at her window was a feature of the neighborhood, and all would agree she was seldom unoccupied.

But today, rolling down the autostrada, skirting the foot of

Vesuvius, passing Pompeii, free for a few hours to reflect, she succumbed to her inherited daydream, now suddenly revived. Later, after running into Professor Haley and experiencing the events that followed, she would think of her reflections in the bus as having been a premonition: it was uncanny that a message from the Duchess and an encounter with the Professor should so closely coincide.

The word the other day from the "Duchess"—in her mind Melba enclosed the word in quotation marks, for though her sister-in-law flaunted the title beside the Great Lakes, she was for Melba merely a rich, middle-class stray, dimly linked to the family by all-but-forgotten matrimony—the first direct word from her in years, had actually been eight words: an eight-word sneer scribbled on a clipping: "See how the precious pictures are treasured now!" The clipping, illustrated with a photograph, said among other things:

> ... Asked further concerning rumors that recent sales have included several paintings from the Jason Deming collection of Italian masters, the trustee refused to confirm or deny the reports ... Recent visitors to the university's art gallery have reported that a number of the Deming pictures are missing from their usual places on the walls. ...

It was natural, Melba supposed, that the Duchess should still hate the pictures. It hadn't taken her long after the wedding to grasp the connection the Roviglianos made between her mid-western millions and the midwestern theft on which they blamed their straitened circumstances. The Duca enjoyed pointing out the connection to his bride. He thought it humorous: the bride could perhaps be pardoned for differing.

Soon it became known that there would be no children. Melba was sure that her sister-in-law had been aware of her own sterility. She had been a hospital nurse, even though a volunteer, and it was common knowledge that hospital nurses were not left in ignorance of intimate matters by their inevitable doctor-lovers. A sterile woman's acceptance of a suitor with a title to pass on was unforgivable. As though in defiance, to prove that the fault was not his, the Duca proceeded to engender by-blows, and did not keep their existence secret. Surely a normal reaction for a man who had been tricked; but the cause of many a loud complaint from the Duchess, who showed herself a prude as well as a non-breeder. The question of annulment never arose, for on one side the title would have had to be relinquished, and on the other—equally unpalatable—the dowry canceled. Italy's entry into the Second World War on what almost everybody later agreed was the wrong side conveniently excused the Duchess's exit "for the duration." That was now so long ago that Melba couldn't remember whether anyone had really expected her to return.

The Duchess's American lawyers had scrupulously remitted what the marriage contract called for: a quarterly sum providentially adjusted to variations in the cost of living. Even when war might have interfered, money arrived regularly, through Switzerland. And even after it became evident that the Duchess herself was gone for good, she wrote an occasional letter, cool but civil. Until . . .

One way of looking at it was that Professor Nathaniel Haley had a lot to answer for. It was after his book appeared and certain of its results became apparent that the Duchess stopped writing. And then the Duca died, and she came and sealed up the salotto. Now there was this clipping—a belated reprise of the old bitterness.

For a real member of the family, the clipping revived other resentments. Melba well remembered a letter quoted in Professor Haley's book which showed that toward the end of his life poor Jason Deming had tried to discover some good in the disaster that had befallen him. "At least," he wrote to a friend, "the pictures hang permanently in a place where the public, and particularly students, can enjoy them." And another letter contained a different attempt at self-consolation: "I must remember that the preservation of the collection as an entity, criminally though it was accomplished, is a permanent tribute to my taste and perseverance."

Now a second swindle was compounding the first. Not only had the family birthright been confiscated by a conscienceless and faceless Institution, but the monument to Jason Deming was being dismantled, its elements wantonly dispersed among a number of equally conscienceless and faceless individuals.

Who were they?

Against those unknown new owners of Deming pictures, Melba, in the bus approaching Salerno, had felt her anger flame much as her parents' and grandparents' had burned against the Institution. Criminals! Buyers of stolen goods!

17

From the Salerno bus station Melba made her way, that day, toward the marketplace.

This was a long open rectangle at the southern edge of the city: the salt truck, coming from Sicily, could enter it without having to cross the center of town. Since the schedule called for the driver to reach Naples by six in the evening, the Salerno stop would probably be made by mid-afternoon. But the run up the peninsula from the ferry terminal at Reggio might be unexpectedly fast or slow: police alerts might cancel scheduled stops on the direct route or dictate long, delaying detours; so there was no telling when the truck would arrive. Her instructions were to wait in the marketplace until it came, or until dark. After delivering her message, or after nightfall, she was free. All this Signor Vispo explained.

For the first time, he had taken her into his confidence, revealed some of the circumstances. "If the truck reaches Naples, our obligations under a new contract will force us to . . . to interfere with it. And with its driver. We should greatly prefer to avoid this, having learned by telephone that the driver on this particular delivery is the brother-in-law of one of us. We all know him. He is a stubborn, foolish boy. We have already spared him a few times. He, or the boss for whom he rashly continues to drive, is counting on our sparing him yet again. To do him justice, he may no longer be doing his work willingly, but out of fear of reprisal should he stop. In any case, he'll now have fair warning not to come to Naples again on salt business. If we fail to convince him, why then I'm afraid that despite family ties . . ."

Melba listened to her employer in silence, but not without thoughts. A business contract more sacrosanct than family! Cold refusal to spare one of one's own more than "a few times"! Why, it might be said that her sister-in-law by the Great Lakes, outlander if ever there was one, was displaying, in allowing her and Laddie to stay in the palazzo, greater family feeling than Signor Vispo and the Club, Neapolitans of Naples. She could see that she was not being dispatched on her errand of mercy with any great enthusiasm. Signor Vispo's customary send-off—"We're counting on you, Principessa, to do your usual splendid best!"—was not bestowed on her today. "Interference!" And with a sister's husband! Perhaps in the Club room itself? She had never forgotten something once heard: a few moments of screaming up there, rising above the throbbing of the jukebox and abruptly suppressed.

Reaching the marketplace, Melba prayed for success.

18

THERE WAS TIME for lunch.

Sitting over her coffee in a trattoria full of market people—like herself they had been up since before dawn—she could no longer keep her eyes open. She felt herself nod; and the next thing she heard was that unlovely waking-sound, half-snore half-snort, and recognized it as her own. Self-consciously she looked about her: no one had heard, for all those who had been sitting near her were gone. There was a buzzing of flies, a murmur of voices from the kitchen. How much time had passed? She glanced at her watch. After two! Hastily she called the waiter and paid. She withdrew, splashed cold water on her face, felt better, and walked out.

In a corner of the marketplace, otherwise empty and somnolent, a small crowd had gathered behind a truck that had not been there before. The truck was gray, unmarked except for its Palermo license plate: as described. The back, when she edged around to it, was open: two young men were standing on the let-down tailpiece. In response to demands from the crowd for "One kilo! Two kilos! Five! Ten!," one was calling out prices and handling money, the other passing down blue parcels. It was a noisy scene, everyone calling at once: the selling must have just started.

Melba stood watching and listening. Which of the two men was the driver? Of him she had been given no description; Signor Vispo had not said there would be a second man. After a few moments she addressed the woman beside her. "This is my first time. Aren't they early? I was told to come a little later."

The woman winked. "Not too much later. Siesta time is so convenient. For the police, I mean. How can they be expected to know what's going on when they're asleep? They're paid well to sleep well. One would have to up the bidding to wake them."

"Always the same two men?"

"No, not always the same driver, even. Whoever it is asks one of us to get up there and give him a hand." The woman peered at the man passing the packages. "I don't know that one. My husband helped once. It earned him a kilo."

Of course: the driver would be the man handling the money.

Some of the customers who had been served were walking away with their blue parcels, others staying to chat and watch. The helper whispered something into the driver's ear, jumped down and disappeared behind a nearby booth.

Now Melba concentrated on the man she had come to warn. He was slight, light-haired like so many descendants of Sicily's Norman conquerors. To Melba he had a special aspect—that of a member of a family meriting greater family protection than was being offered him. A deplorable tendency today: she knew that her own concern would be total, were one of her relations in danger. Left alone, the young smuggler was continuing to call out prices and made change, stepping back into the truck from time to time to bring out the parcels demanded.

The helper did not return. The driver began to cast glances in the direction he had taken. The glances, always expressionless, grew more frequent; became, for a long moment, a steady stare; and then abruptly, his face still unchanging, without a word to anyone, Melba's unwitting protégé jumped to the ground. As the crowd murmured, he quickly lifted and slammed shut the heavy tailpiece, its chains clanking, and began, now feverishly, to pull-to the double doors above it. But it was too late. The wail of a siren came not from a distance, but screamingly loud and from very close: the car must have crept silently down nearby streets, and now it burst into view. The crowd had to scatter before it; women shrieked, calling on the Madonna. In an instant three policemen were out.

It was an undramatic arrest, if any arrest can be undramatic. The driver put up no argument, did not resist the handcuffs. The crowd stood watching; silent at first, it broke into mocking laughter when the policeman assigned to drive the truck away failed to get it started and had to ask the handcuffed driver to do it for him.

Truck and police car disappeared.

19

IF THAT HAD BEEN the whole of Melba's experience in Salerno, she would have been less agitated when she met Nat in the street a few hours later. She would have been anxious even so, for having missed her contact she would have feared that the driver, if by some overbidding of his own he had succeeded in getting himself and his truck released by the police, would be continuing unwarned to Naples, arriving there late, perhaps, but surely in time for "interference" by the Committee. But she did not allow her mission to end there.

From the marketplace she made her way to the center of the city, asking directions, and came finally to police headquarters. She saw the gray truck parked in the courtyard, and entering she asked the duty officer at the desk to be allowed to speak to the driver just recently brought in.

The officer lowered his radio. "Impossible, Signora. Who are you?"

"I am his godmother, and a nun."

"A nun!"

"I know what you are thinking and looking at. Surely you know that the Holy Father allows us, in these modern times, to dress as we please when we go out into the world?"

"Have you identification?"

"Certainly."

It was a splendidly engraved card.

Suora Maria Teresa
dei Principi di Castiglia-Miranda

Madre Superiore del Convento
del Divino Amore, Napoli

Once a year, on her feast day, it came accompanying a gift of convent-made glacé fruit from her childhood friend and distant cousin Terry. (Nickname bestowed by the inevitable English nanny.)

She herself had often longed, after the collapse of several marriage prospects, to take the veil rather than remain her brother's housekeeper. The difficulty was that not just any convent would do. Only certain orders, certain communities, were suitable for one of her rank; and proper convents, like proper husbands, demanded more of a dowry than she could muster. She was welcomed as a visitor at any number, where the Mother Superior and various of the nuns were often relations or school friends. But as for joining ... Regrets, usually affectionate, sometimes even tearful, but always firm, were invariably expressed when she had to mention the sum her brother said was all he could afford. She knew quite well that he had made it low because it was to his advantage to keep her at home. Then another use for that small sum had arisen—she had not regretted what it had enabled her to do for the boy Pasquale—and there was nothing left. Subsequently, the advent of Laddie had changed everything—the unexpected infant who had turned her into a mother when all hope of motherhood was extinguished. A convent might come later, when the fund was no longer needed.

"A moment. I will see what I can do, Altezza."

Approximately three minutes later—it was now about three o'clock—Melba was sure she had rescued the young driver from grievous injury, so obvious was it that at the announcement of Terry's name the police had stopped what they were doing to him. They brought him out quickly, after washing off some of the blood. They said nothing—just looked embarrassed. In the background she caught a glimpse of one of their superiors, peering from his office to have a look at her. She knew better, as Terry, than to be shrill, or to show horror. A few stern words: "Someone will hear of this. Call us a taxi." When it came, the young man followed her dumbly.

As the hospital pointed out, an hour or so later, when they refused to keep him, he was "ambulatory"; and the ambulatory were not given beds. But Melba knew they recognized the source of his injuries and wanted him out of the way. They had been wary from the moment she appeared with him in the emergency room. They had demanded no identification from either of them, and she had thought it best to offer none.

Yes, he had been surprised by the treatment given him, he told her, as still battered and bruised but now bandaged he sat with her in a bar. He had always been told that Salerno was safe. In fact his attempt to close the truck and get away had been in part to make things easier for the police. Even when the handcuffs were snapped on he had had no fear. But whoever had overbid his boss must have been lavish, for when at headquarters he had offered what *he* had—and it was no small sum, the proceeds of sales all the way up from Reggio—they sneered and struck. When Melba asked "Who could that overbidder be?," he grinned at her—he was feeling better now, with two brandies inside him, and making a show of pretending that what had happened was all part of the game. He was a tough, blond bantam of a Sicilian, some of his dialect hard for her to understand.

"Signora, your warning comes from my brother-in-law and his friends, correct?"

"Of course it comes from them."

"So who would do me in except their opposite numbers here? The Salerno Committee. The job was done down here instead of in Naples, that's all. The difference being that down here they paid the police to do it for them, whereas in Naples they'd have done it themselves." He grinned again.

"Your own family! How dreadful!"

"Oh Signora, what's the difference? It's all the same who does it!"

That was the last of his jauntiness, for at that point he fainted.

When he came to, more or less, on the floor of the bar, with everyone crowding and kind, she called for another taxi. She knew this must be something grave. Into one of his pockets she slipped the printed prayer she always carried with her—the card, blessed by the Pope, calling on the Madonna for succor in times of peril; and back at the hospital she was no longer anonymous and quiet. This time she showed Terry's card, demanded an examination. They wheeled him away. She waited. After a long time a doctor and a nurse appeared. From the way they looked, she might have guessed the news, but she wasn't ready for it. When they told her, she said, with a curious sensation of speaking like an automaton and yet knowing that she was succeeding in sounding imperious: "Kindly leave me alone for a few minutes."

"Perhaps you would like a sedative?"

"Kindly do as I ask."

Casting curious glances, they obeyed.

And she was out of the hospital in a twinkling.

What else to do? Stay to be questioned, admit that she wasn't

Terry? Implicate the Club? The poor boy was dead. No help for him now. He would be identified quickly enough.

She hurried from the hospital quarter, reached the busy shopping promenade, lost herself in the crowd. And ran into Professor Haley, Nat.

She wondered, afterward, what she had said to him. Not too much, she hoped. Though she had a memory of "chattering like a magpie." Wasn't that the English expression, not thought of in years?

That poor boy! Melba was not unacquainted with death. In her swarming old quarter of Naples, in the palazzo-tenement itself, she was frequently called to the bedsides of dying or dead neighbors who, or whose families, were grateful for a last visit from the Principessa. But in the second taxi, when she had held the half-conscious young Sicilian in her arms, tried to ease him, brushed the blond hair from his eyes, it was no mere performance of an act of mercy; this was what it would be like to have a stricken Laddie beside her.

Despite the financial strain, and in the face of Signor Vispo's frequent reminders to her, and to Laddie himself, that assignments could be his for the asking, she had never suggested to Laddie that he too work for the Club. When Laddie had recently volunteered, although she had not attempted to dissuade him—she saw the enlistment as part of his new restlessness and obstinacy—she had exacted from Vispo a promise of safety. Perhaps if today's Sicilian hadn't been young and slight and blond; if his struggles to put his dialect into proper Italian for her understanding hadn't reminded her of Laddie's hesitations when they spoke English; perhaps then her revulsion against the Club would not have swollen to the proportions it had as the bus approached Naples. When she descended, she felt sick; when she reached her own house, she had to force herself to enter it. Once inside, discipline led her straight upstairs to the Club room.

There was some relief in finding Signor Vispo there alone—in not having to see the others. There was more in discovering that no accounting would be required of her. Not that she could have given one, at first. Everything blurred, she stumbled; Signor Vispo sprang to her, helped her into a chair just in time, and in a moment was ministering to her as she had to the Sicilian. "I know all about it, Principessa," from a kind of darkness she heard him say. "I have had a report by telephone. Put your head down, down. Lower, Principessa, lower. Now, sniff this." Sharp fumes rose. "Sniff, Principessa." Salts. Ammonia salts. Kept there in the Club for visitors in need of revival following strain of one kind or another.

Recovering, she learned that a member of the Salerno Committee had been watching throughout. Watching the truck, watching his fellow member the "helper," watching the arrest; and watching *her*, from the moment she had shown herself interesting by entering the police station. He had telephoned the story to Naples, reporting with pride the discipline Salerno had meted out. The response had shocked him. For Naples, on learning the details, had exploded. "I exploded, Principessa. I have already told the Consortium that the unnecessary fatality has strained the loyalty of one of our best members here in Naples. Salerno itself must be disciplined. Friction between Committees can only increase the risk . . ."

"Increase the risk!" Melba's voice rose. "You said there was no risk! Where is Ladi? He must be recalled! I want to see him, here! He must not . . ."

"Principessa!" With a bound he was at the jukebox, and she flinched from instant blare. Now he had to shout. "The strain, Principessa. I know. I am sorry. Wait. I can relieve it." He went to the telephone, dialed, turned his back. He spoke a few words, there was a long wait; then he faced her, beckoned, handed her the receiver, turned down the music.

Laddie sounded nearby, utterly himself, perfectly calm. Yes, of course all was well. Why shouldn't it be? Everything was going according to plan. Vispo said she was a little upset. Why?

She forced herself to speak evenly. "I felt a need for reassurance."

"Then be reassured. No reason not to be. I'll see you in a few days. Okay?"

The quick little "okay" was the most reassuring part of it. She knew better than to ask where he was. "Good-bye, then. Till soon."

She hung up. "Thank you." How quickly she was back in pace—a skittish horse brought under control, resuming its trot between the shafts!

"Is there someone you could have with you tonight, Principessa? Someone to look after you a little? I appreciate the shock you have had. If you like, I could ask . . ."

"No, no." Couldn't he sense her present revulsion from anything or anyone that he or the Club might provide? A respite from the Club and all it connoted: that was all she wanted. "Might there be less noise tonight, please?"

He promised to keep the place silent.

Downstairs. Around the walled-up salotto to the bedroom she had left before dawn. Exhaustion. It seemed a very long time before she could turn out the light. For once she didn't even hear the rats.

THE BANKNOTE she found in an envelope slipped under her door in the morning, though not blood money, was nevertheless larger, she was sure, than had there been no blood. Not a bonus for success this time: failure was complete. It was compensation for an ordeal; and whereas her other Club money had been deposited with satisfaction, she took this to the bank without joy.

20

O<small>N</small> S<small>UNDAY</small> she was gripped by a newspaper headline which she might ordinarily have ignored.

SALTY EPISODE IN VIA ROMA

Last evening a quartet of American crew members from a large yacht anchored off our city experienced a rude surprise shortly after disembarking at Landing Stage No. 2 in the New Basin. And just when Naples seemed to be extending them a warm welcome!

Met, apparently according to pre-arrangement, by Colonel X. (U.S. Army), from the NATO base, they were introduced by him to the Italian Customs officials on duty, and on his recommendation given courtesy-clearance: i.e., their effects were not examined, even though they were carrying parcels of considerable bulk. After thanking the obliging Customs men they were driven off by the Colonel in his luxurious green Chevrolet.

A few minutes later they presented themselves at a well-known tabaccheria in Via Roma, where the proprietor himself, Signor Y., happened to be alone, just about to close the shop. One of the Americans suggested that in view of the current shortage of salt, Signor Y. (who speaks impeccable English) might wish to take advantage of "a fantastic opportunity." After viewing and tasting the sample offered, which proved to be an excellent grade of Sicilian, Signor Y. offered to telephone a colleague who, he said, might be willing to participate in the transaction. The quartet's spokes-man "reminded" Signor Y. that if by any chance it was the police he intended to call, it would be pointless, as they had "protection." This was a clear reference to the Colonel, who had remained outside in the Chevrolet. Denying any such intention, Signor Y. made his call; and within a very short space of time there arrived on the scene not, in fact, the police, but . . .

We are not at liberty to reveal the identities of the civic-spirited citizens who rallied so promptly to the cause of legality. Posing as the tobacconist's "colleague," their chief of operations entered the shop, and being of a persuasive temperament soon established his *bona fides*. During the ensuing discussion of "terms" he succeeded in distracting the group's attention from the street and the Chevrolet-storehouse. The surprise of the Americans was considerable when at a lull in the "negotiations" this was found to have silently vanished from its parking place, Colonel and all!

Before the indignant quartet had time to draw the firearms they were discovered to be carrying, they found themselves outnumbered by the troop of equally well-armed vigilantes, who, having waited the while without, posing as loungers (incidentally screening the abduction of the Chevrolet and the Colonel by others of their number), now entered the shop in support of their leader. Seeing that insistence was useless, the discomfited—and disarmed—would-be smugglers de-parted, muttering vague threats (it was all they could do) of "getting even."

It is said that the owners of the yacht, persons of con-siderable prominence . . .

But Melba was not interested in the owners of the yacht. She was agitated by the words "getting even," especially since from her window she could see, parked in a corner of the palazzo courtyard, a green American automobile never there before.

Late that afternoon, when she was at her window again, Signor Vispo entered the courtyard from the street, looked up, and made a gesture combining greeting with "May I see you?" Inside, he said, "I bring good news." And pointing to her newspaper, still open to SALTY EPISODE: "Do you think of me as having a 'persuasive temperament,' Principessa? Incidentally, let me relieve your mind about the poor tool of a Colonel. He was dropped a few doors from his home, safe and sound. Maybe the episode will teach NATO not to assign officers to do every last thing the Kaloumians want, all-important though NATO may think the Kaloumians are."

"The Kaloumians? Are they involved?" Not being in the *Libro d'oro*, the famous pair were known to Melba only as they were to countless other women—from magazines seen at the hairdresser's.

"Not the Kaloumians personally, Principessa. Much too small a matter for them. Their crew. That is, their servants. The Kaloumians think the chief function of NATO is to keep their servants happy. The Kaloumians' crew think of themselves as tough characters, and perhaps they are, on their own ground. Of course here in Naples they're indescribably, irresistibly innocent."

The good news he had come to deliver was, first, that Don Ladislao, never in "actual danger," was now "in an absolutely secure place, one hundred percent out of harm's way." She had no cause for worry whatever.

Melba wished she knew just where it was that Laddie was spending Sunday afternoon so safely.

Second: "On Tuesday I'll take you to see him. We'll travel on the same hydrofoil, but separately, and converge at the proper place. Take an overnight bag. The hotel will be deluxe. I have already reserved your room. And in preparation . . ." Signor Vispo hesitated. It was unusual for him to hesitate. "In preparation, Principessa, perhaps you would allow me to offer you a new costume? Please forgive me. You always look most distinguished. It's just that hotels of that category . . ."

She tightened her lips against laughter. Vispo—Pasquale—telling her to dress up! The clothes—if they could be called clothes—he'd been wearing when he arrived at the palazzo fresh from the apricots! His thirteen-year-old pride, almost to bursting, when she helped him on with his first houseboy jacket! Now as he counted out bills from his wallet, a yearning for finery gave way to regret at squandering the money instead of swelling the fund. But of course there would be a fee besides.

"If I am to buy clothes, you must tell me where I'll be wearing them."

He told her. The Imperatore! Her brother and his bride had spent their honeymoon there. Years ago. Family and wedding guests had seen them off at the steamer. No hydrofoil then. Even longer ago she herself had spent a night on the island, taken by her parents to celebrate a childhood birthday. So Laddie was there now . . . She didn't ask Signor Vispo what her work was to be. What difference did it make? By not breaking away from the Club, by keeping silent about a murder at Salerno, she had declared herself available for anything.

In the course of Signor Vispo's Monday briefing she learned the details of Laddie's duties on the island. He had "distracted a watchman's attention" during one operation and "acted as a red herring" following another; in each case facilitating the performance and getaway of members of the Club.

"Mrs. Kaloumian will join the yacht at the island tomorrow evening," she also learned. "We are sure of that, thanks to the Rome Committee. They found out yesterday she's chartered a seaplane to take her there. The yacht itself will arrive much earlier. It's like the stories you used to tell me, Principessa, about how everybody and everything always had to be ready and waiting for hours whenever Royalty was expected. With most of their cargo still to get rid of, the crew will want to give themselves plenty of time. I'd expect them around noon. We've been able to slip them the name of the best place on the island to try, and I have no doubt they'll show up there."

That was only part of the program. Before turning out her light she went over the rest of it.

Had she put everything into the overnight case, into her handbag? From the handbag one thing was of course missing. Until she had slipped it into the young Sicilian's pocket, the little card blessed by the Pope, with the prayer for the Madonna's protection, had always accompanied her. She wondered where it was now. She must send for another. Meanwhile, a substitute talisman. Some other image of Mary, her protectress. She found one: indeed it was in her handbag already. She had not thought it would be asked to fill such a role.

21

THE PRESIDENT of the Hotel and Restaurant Keepers' Association of the island, who happened that year to be the manager of the Imperatore, had called an emergency meeting for Tuesday morning. He had telephoned each member the evening before; and shortly before nine they began to assemble. The Imperatore's television room, ordinarily empty at that hour, gradually filled. As nine o'clock struck in the piazza clock tower the president-manager glanced out a window commanding a view of the port. "In about ten minutes, Gentlemen. The hydrofoil is just docking." He then went out into the lobby.

Almost exactly ten minutes later he was seen to greet, and to accompany to the reception desk, a quietly but smartly dressed older woman who had just arrived, her overnight case, surprisingly shabby in comparison with her costume, carried by the Imperatore's baggageman who met guests at the pier. The next arrival, a gentleman with a notably long nose, the president-manager escorted directly to the television room. The newcomer indicated his preference for a seat at the rear. The president-manager declared the meeting open, and conveyed the regrets of the single absent member, the manager of Swank, who had telephoned that an emergency was keeping him away.

The association was easy in its internal workings, the island's major and minor hotels, pensions and restaurants being realistic regarding their respective categories; and today they sufficiently suspected the nature of the agenda to recognize that the spotlight would necessarily be on the two largest among them, with preference given to the Imperatore (De Luxe) over the Albergo New-York (First Class).

"You will have noticed, Gentlemen, that we have with us this morning no representatives of either local or national law-enforcement agencies." So began the president-manager.

"Law-enforcement"! No laughter or smiles greeted that phrase, nor had the speaker expected any. It had not been uttered ironically, for it would never have occurred to the islanders that "enforcement" meant anything but its opposite—much as the "refineries" at Naples polluted an entire province. Daily, the laden spider fleet was seen returning from international waters under the gaze of revenue-service helicopters. Those islanders who owned grottoes and rented them out as fueling stations to the spiders observed a kind of honor system, turning over approximately a tithe of that income directly to the local Commissariat; from which convenient collection point the total was known to be shared with the helicopter patrol, and no doubt with other enforcers of the law.

"That is because those agencies are already cognizant of the announcements I shall make. The first is this. As the result of incessant negotiations both direct and telephonic, certain disciplinary measures initiated on this island have come to an end. With the approval of myself and my colleague from the Albergo-New York, official investigations of recent events that have involved all of us have been dropped. The inspectors from Rome have returned to Rome. None of you need fear any incidents on your premises if you will follow a proposed procedure to which we ourselves have agreed."

As the president-manager paused, only a few of the assembled members succeeded in restraining themselves from twisting round to take another look at the stranger. No one now failed to realize whose representative he was, just as no one failed to understand the force of the word "proposed."

"What has happened, Gentlemen, is that the island has a new, responsible supplier. There will be no more of those haphazard deliveries from Sicily. Henceforth our salt will come from a single controlled Sardinian source."

Silence.

Everyone in the audience admired the Consortium for the way it had won its salt victory on the island: speed, minimal violence, no bloodshed. The humbler members liked its use of two of the island's three upper-category establishments as scapegoats: those very hotels which, in their lavish use of highly taxed salt water for their pools, had openly proclaimed themselves major salt consumers. The third, Swank, had long been rumored to be owned, like the spider fleet, by the Consortium itself. That it alone remained undamaged was now recognized as transforming rumor into fact; and its manager's absence from the meeting was seen as tactful. His having instituted a baggage-search when he knew himself to be invulnerable was both shrewd and seemly.

"One point the new supplier wishes to make very clear. In the warehouse it will open as soon as its first shipment arrives, sale will be direct to consumer. Purchase from any other source is to be avoided. Resale at a markup by individual or group is equally to be avoided: there is no place on this island for a middleman."

"Intermediario"—"middleman." But those listening carefully had heard the manager change the final *o*, the masculine vowel, to *a*. "Middlewoman": and they knew he meant Madre Serafina.

"Ponder, Signori. The new situation requires pondering. I invite suggestions."

No one quite knew how the Mother Superior had made herself the intermediaria. Had she threatened the Revenue Service, the Commissariat? Threatened to expose their connections with the Consortium's spider fleet and its drug-running, for instance? But to whom could she do her exposing who didn't know all about such things already, and were themselves both protectors and protected?

The explanation could only be more subtle. A matter of personality. She was one of the deep ones. An uncanny, cussed, witch-like type, with emanations that gave her ascendancy. Those eyes of hers! That voice, and her willingness to use it. As legal salt had dwindled because of the strike, incoming contraband, always from Sicily, had found its way to her from the beginning. How so? She seemed simply to have been there to seize the opportunity, and no one had come forward to oppose her. Everyone knew her need for money: everyone sympathized with her in her feud with the Parroco and his discotheque church. But even if they hadn't, would it have made any difference? Large orders for hotels and restaurants, small orders for families—all had been efficiently filled by her busy nuns. And now . . .

"Ponder, Gentlemen. And if no decision is reached before this meeting is closed, continue to ponder, and we will meet again. Remember: the intermediaria is of now eliminated. Eliminated as intermediaria, I mean, of course. Perhaps a vacuum has been created. And they say a vacuum is dangerous. The question is: are there measures we can take to prevent her causing serious disturbance in our community?"

While the president-manager was speaking, a single church bell had begun the traditional slow, mournful tolling that announced the funeral of a deceased islander. Around the room there was a flickering of hands as members—and the visiting stranger—crossed themselves. The bell fell silent, and was duly followed, according to the Parroco's new practice, by an electronic requiem:

> *Somewhere, over the Rainbow,*
> *Way up High . . .*

As it ended, there was a sound at the back of the room. The stranger had risen. He nodded to the president-manager, gestured toward himself and toward the door. The president-manager hurried to open it for him, and with a bow to all he was gone.

THAT WOULD keep them thinking awhile.

Small communities were all the same. Delighted to believe that their little problems were of consequence. Was Madre Serafina really an extraordinary force of nature, as his scouts had reported her to be considered locally? The important thing, to Vispo, was that she was so considered. His warning (included in his telephonic negotiations with the Imperatore and the Albergo) that the village witch would have to be coped with had flattered them all. They loved being asked to cope, to "ponder." And while they pondered, he himself would solve the problem of the old strega in a twinkling. It would be well worth the price in cash to ensure the smooth working of the new order, and to show the islanders yet again—though by now they scarcely needed another demonstration—what the Consortium was made of. And of course to show the Consortium, his new employers, what he, Vispo, was made of.

Having hitherto acted only for lesser individuals and organizations, Vispo had had to accustom himself to the idiosyncrasies of the very powerful: e.g., the chiefs of the Consortium. He had persuaded them he was qualified, by long residence on Sardinia, to deal with the chain of salt refineries recently and hastily brought under Consortium control there. (He could imagine some of the methods used.) The strike of the Italian state refiners meant that the entire Italian peninsula was legally saltless—deprived, in a way, of its virility. Much quick money was to be made by contraband, with only ill-organized Sicilian competition to contend with. Vispo had thought the Consortium padroni would be enraged by the Nessiemen's impudent salt foray in Via Roma; but to his surprise they had reacted with glee, flattered by this challenge from individuals close to the famous Kaloumian, a grander, more international version of themselves. And when Vispo told them the crew's attempt was sure to be repeated on the island, where he was planning to contain it again, they were like the owners of a football team on the eve of a match. Vispo knew that salt was a mere sideline for the Consortium—the crystals and powders regularly transported by its spider fleet were more precious and more lethal; nevertheless, a number of members had announced their intention of being present at the island salt confrontation. Several, who must have left Rome at dawn, were on the early hydrofoil Vispo had taken with Melba.

Concerning Melba, Vispo knew that he had one cause for uncertainty. Could she be relied on not to go to pieces should she see her darling Ladislao in a situation of even ordinary risk? On the other hand, how darling was Ladislao to Melba? Any computer, fed the requirements and circumstances of this new assignment, would come up with her name as the ideal agent—*if* she was not anxious about the boy to the point of instability. Sometimes it seemed that her devotion to him was a close second to her wild ancestral fixation. At other times, a very far second. In Salerno her emotions had for the first time got the better of her. She should have headed back to Naples the minute she saw the young Sicilian arrested. Nothing had been accomplished by her attempts at rescue. Vispo wondered to what extent devotion to Ladislao had inspired those attempts. It might be interesting to put her to a test.

In Palazzo Rovigliano Melba was respected, even loved, by the humbler tenants. To them she was kind, in a feudal way. The ones in the better flats she quickly snubbed if they showed any tendency toward what she considered familiarity; to them she was condescending, never hesitating to remind them how fortunate they were to inhabit her palazzo. Even the humbler tenants laughed at her, but she was a candidate for their pity, as well. In Naples, eccentrics and irrationals are usually found endearing, and sympathy is extended to them if they are thought to be exploited or victimized. Ladislao, too, was a courtyard favorite. Vispo knew the tenants were watching.

He enjoyed being on the island. He considered his short visit something of a holiday. Staying at the Imperatore was part of it. Living as Duca had lived, when Duca could still afford it. Today *he* could afford it.

Time, now, for him to set off for Swank with Melba.

22

THE SIGHT of Laddie sitting at Swank's gate as she and Vispo arrived brought a pair of words to Melba's lips from out of the past—from the days when the girls at the Sacred Heart made Latin responses at Mass: "Deo gratias." She restricted herself to the usual kiss on both cheeks, however, and Laddie said, "Hello yourself." That expression had taken his fancy on NATO radio, and he and she used it between them.

Behind her and Vispo, early customers were waiting to enter, and as they passed through the gate she heard Laddie doing his job, politely asking to be allowed to look at the newcomers' beach bags. At the counter Vispo presented the manager; they continued on, threading their way among the deck chairs surrounding the pool. If

Vispo hadn't told her to expect them, she might not have recognized the several members of the Club wearing only bathing slips and dark glasses, stretched out like Swank's other customers, taking the sun. Then, in the dim, bamboo-sheltered bar-restaurant, Vispo ordered coffee for them both, took a newspaper from his briefcase, and said they would "await developments."

After a little while there was the sound of raised American voices out toward the gate. She heard the manager mention Laddie, and the noise subsided.

Then, quite a while later, Laddie came quietly in under the bamboo. As he murmured a few words to Vispo she was all in readiness, thinking that now her work would begin. But Vispo, standing up, motioned to her to stay where she was. "A totally unconnected, minor episode, Principessa. I'll not be long." He and Laddie went off. And indeed he was soon back, and back in his newspaper.

Though sitting with her at a table, he still wore his hat. He had retained a number of crudities absorbed from his adoptive parents. They had been a respectable couple, much the best of those who had answered her advertisement offering, in return for legal adoption, the small sum her brother had allowed. Quite nicely far away, too—in Sardinia. Nobody had expected Pasquale to return to Naples, and certainly not as an experienced buyer and seller of protection.

Suddenly, from somewhere on Swank's premises, came shouts that were more like roars, human roars. "Doesn't concern us," said Vispo, barely looking up. "Think nothing of it."

But the roaring persisted, and spread—became a tumult, the cries of a crowd, the crowd of bathers and sunbathers just outside the door. From her seat Melba could see people running, deck chairs overturned. Agitation seized her. "Laddie!" she cried, jumping up; and to Vispo: "You promised there'd be no violence!"

"A sideshow, Principessa. I promise you, just a sideshow. No danger whatever. Please be calm."

When she ran to the door he took her by the arm—something he had never done before; she pulled herself free; and there, outside, was chaos. And Professor Haley—again. Barely a minute later came the sound of Laddie's whistling.

A POLICE BOAT arrived at Swank fairly quickly in response to the manager's telephone call, and within a few minutes the skipper of the *Gattopardo II* was handcuffed and taken away, as any salt-smuggler properly should be in a law-abiding republic. Several of the Consortium's chiefs, who had now joined Swank's regular customers and the Club members in deck chairs around the pool, complacently watched the disposal of the interloping Sicilian and his wares. Vispo was not sorry to have his employers witness the demonstration of his efficiency. The stage, cluttered by that unexpected incident, had to be cleared, for the *Nessie*, now anchored in deep waters offshore, would soon be lowering her dinghy for the foolhardy delivery of yet more doomed Sicilian merchandise.

Not that Swank's premises were totally quiet even after the luckless skipper left.

Considering that all their travel-possessions except their bathing suits and what they had in their bathhouses had gone down with the ship, the party of six Americans were perhaps behaving normally; but they were not silent. At first they had been very loud indeed, almost as loud as the skipper himself, and after a quick conference between Vispo and the manager the latter approached them, accompanied by Melba, and assured them in his best English of Swank's concern for their plight. "This here lady" would soon be going to the village, where she would be glad to shop for them and do what else she could to help with emergency restitution.

Melba, thus snatched from Professor Haley, to whom she had just begun to introduce Laddie, stepped as calmly as she could into this new role assigned her, virtually that of shop assistant. "What is the most pressing requirement, Mesdames?"

Being upset, the girls were testy at first.

"In this day and age she has to ask, yet."

"The whole supply down the drink."

"And the Pope says nix."

Small thanks to Nanny's English-teaching that Melba's perplexity was brief. Her greatest coup with them was her promise to secure an adequate supply that very afternoon from the island pharmacy—which, she assured the girls, like all Italian pharmacies except perhaps the one in the Vatican itself, ignored Papal edicts. Later, at home, as they showed their slides, they would say to friends: "The Princess—we discovered she was a Princess—was very gracious to us." And they sometimes added: "When the boys told her they were veterans of Salerno she smiled, graciously, and said that in a way she was one herself. We assumed she meant she'd been living there during the landings, but she was so gracious and such an aristocrat we didn't like to pry."

Melba's shopping list grew quite long, what with the sextet interrupting each other as they thought of more indispensables. By telephone the manager made reservations for them at the Imperatore.

23

"You do quite resemble your aunt."

The American Professor said that, following Melba's interrupted "This is my nephew . . ." when she was called away.

Ladislao reflected that the Professor could have no idea of the turbulence his remark would have roused only a few days before. "You think so?" he said. "Perhaps. I've never thought about it."

Ladislao quickly regretted that cold and untruthful answer. Recent turmoil had left him raw; besides, circumstances were awkward. The Professor, whose name he had known all his life, seemed to be allied with the invertito. They had come together to the jail, and here they were together again at Swank.

The invertito was the American of Sunday.

His own assignment had been, that Sunday, to be found by the police "skulking suspiciously" near the Albergo New-York, so that they would stop, ask questions, and probably arrest him. That would give the workmen from the Club more time to get away. But the chance meeting with the invertito, and the smirking, compromising way the invertito behaved when the police appeared, had resulted in his being held on two counts—not only that of involvement in the explosions, which he had been prepared for. How stupidly the police had grinned at them both! That humiliation he now saw as the culmination of his trouble: indeed its very acuteness had actuated the cure.

Ladislao was further sobered by the exultation in Vispo's voice the next day, when, having learned of the soliciting charge, he ironically thanked him for "service beyond the call of duty." The two assignments—the distraction of the Imperatore's watchman, and the skulking near the New-York—had been accepted duty: parts of his job with the Club—the job he had asked for following the onset of confusion. After performing such services, and especially considering the humiliation, it was natural to try to avoid or ignore the other persons involved; and in the jail he had accomplished just that. But it was scarcely possible here and now, when the Professor said: "I didn't quite hear your name. This is my friend Lyle Brennan."

Ladislao watched the Professor hesitate before making that introduction. Then he did it in a seemly way. As Ladislao and the invertito shook hands, the invertito laughed: that was natural enough, perhaps: in the jail, his motive in offering to "pay for a lawyer" and other services had been transparent. (There had of course been no need for defense: a telephone call from Vispo to the island Commissariat the same evening had opened the steel doors.) The Professor was obviously what Melba would call "an American gentleman." A variation of that phrase was what she always used to describe his own partial namesake: Jason Deming had been a "very distinguished American gentleman." A copy of his biography, inscribed by its author, this very Professor, had always been on display in the palazzo. He had often looked at it. Not having been driven to read it by any family passion such as Melba's, he had only recently done so for the first time. Turning the pages brought back his childhood delight in its plates of angels, madonnas, saints and quaint landscapes, but on reading he had found himself resenting the book. Too often, when life was more trying than usual in the palazzo, he had seen Melba take refuge in hysteria about the "theft" of the family pictures; and he blamed the Professor and his book for being her constant reminder.

"I know you're familiar with one of my names, Professor. Deming."

"Deming? Your family name is Deming?"

"No. I am Ladislao Deming Rovigliano."

The Professor hesitated: "Deming can't be a very common name in Italy."

That was clearly a cover for bewilderment. It occurred to him that so far as he knew, Melba and the Professor had never been in touch during his lifetime. Until now the Professor might even have been unaware of his existence. He ignored the invertito—he decided to ignore him from then on—and addressed the Professor as though they were alone.

"I am the son of the Duca."

"I see. Yes, as Melba's nephew you would have to be. Since he was her only brother. And she had no sister, I believe." Pause. "I see: 'Ladislao' from the ancient king of Naples—the family king, you might say." The Professor glanced toward the invertito, as though about to offer some explanation of what he had just said, but apparently decided against it. "And 'Deming' of course because you're partly American." Pause. "But I had always understood that the Duchess . . ." There, for all his brave effort, the poor Professor had to break off and begin again. "When I ran into Melba the other day in Salerno . . ."

"You saw Melba?"

"Yes. In Salerno. We met there by chance. We had a talk. You seem surprised."

"I didn't know she'd been there. She and I have been . . . separated. She hasn't had time to tell me . . ."

"I was about to say that in Salerno she didn't tell *me*. She didn't mention . . ."

At that point the invertito cried, "God, here comes the dinghy!" And without ceremony was gone, running toward the parapet overlooking the landing stage.

Why should the invertito be interested in the *Nessie*'s dinghy? That was the Club's concern. It was just pulling away from the gigantic yacht. Now Vispo would be needing all hands.

"Melba didn't mention *you*," said the Professor.

Everybody knew the drill about the reception of the men from the *Nessie*. According to your assignment, you either stayed where you were or moved inconspicuously to a certain spot. The normal holiday aspect of Swank was to be preserved. That was why the unscheduled hullabaloo about the *Gattopardo II* had worried them. However, the place had become itself again. He knew where to go. "You must excuse me." He saw Professor Haley, by now the very picture of puzzlement, looking after him as he moved to the entrance gate.

24

Sᴵᴛᴛɪɴɢ ᴀᴛ his assigned post, Ladislao watched the approach of the so-called dinghy. A big, ugly, snub-nosed craft, a kind of landing barge to match its grotesque yacht. There were only two men in it besides the helmsman—one of them observing Swank through binoculars, as must already have been done from the yacht itself. Vispo had stayed close to the bar enclosure from the moment the *Nessie* was sighted, lest his face be remembered from the episode in Via Roma. The other Club members on duty here today had been chosen from among those who had not participated in that scene. Ladislao and the manager, who would be the first to receive the approaching guests, were equally unknown to them.

The dinghy reached the landing stage. The *Nessie* had been recognized by Swank's magazine-reading clientele, and a cluster of watchers gathered on the parapet. There were murmurs of disappointment when it was seen that the two figures being transported were not the Kaloumians. "The Kaloumians' leather-men," someone muttered. Black leather jackets, breeches and boots; a black walkie-talkie bristling with antennae; and there was no doubt about what made the jackets bulge over the—presumed—hearts. As Swank's attendant held the boat fast, the two passengers clambered out. To one of them the helmsman handed up a blue package, and the pair mounted the stairs, glancing about as though wary of ambush. One was young, the other weatherbeaten; each exuded his own brand of tender mercy. A silence fell over the watchers.

Following instructions, Ladislao waved the two men through.

At the counter they stopped. And as the older demanded the manager, awaiting them in his inner office, there was a cry from one of the American sextet. "Pat! Pat Hickey! Jesus Christ! You old shit!"

The leatherman's response was delayed by a moment apparently required for recognition. Then: "Harry! Jesus Christ! You old motherfucker, you!"

And in an instant the male members of the sextet and the leatherman newcomer were in mass embrace. Fists thudded on backs, and Swank reverberated with the name of the Lord taken in vain.

When the huddle loosened, endearments continued intense.

"Pat, you old ———! Jesus Christ!"

"Jesus Christ! After thirty years!"

"Salerno! The old outfit! Jesus Christ!"

"September '43! Jesus Christ!"

"Jesus Christ!"

"Jesus H. Chr . . . !"

Then the delighted girls were included; the younger leatherman accepted his introduction; a circle formed; the blue package and the walkie-talkie were set down and drinks loudly called for. Those who had been watching and listening dispersed. To its ordinary customers, Swank must have seemed once again its normal self.

The manager, emerging, signaled to Ladislao and pointed toward the bar; and for the second time that day Ladislao made his way among the deck chairs to give Vispo news of an unexpected interruption. This one Vispo had watched himself, through chinks in the enclosure, and he merely muttered, "We'll wait. Now send me Melba."

Ladislao had noticed, during recent weeks, that more and more often Vispo said "Melba," rather than "the Principessa" or "your aunt" when the two of them were alone.

MELBA REMAINED in the bar with Vispo for some time, and when she emerged she asked Ladislao to walk with her down to the ferry. "Did you like Professor Haley?"

"He said he ran into you in Salerno. I didn't know you'd been there."

"When could I have told you? On the telephone there wasn't time."

They made their way to the landing stage

"Melba, the Professor said you didn't . . ."

He found he lacked the courage to finish the sentence, to hear himself admit, by saying it aloud, that in Salerno she hadn't mentioned his existence. Besides, the ferryman was ready to leave, was holding out his hand to help her aboard. She murmured, "Promise you'll be careful," and the boat roared off.

He saw that the dinghy was tied loosely, as though for a quick getaway, its black-clad helmsman smoking in his place, looking at no one.

BACK AT the gate, Ladislao didn't see Professor Haley approach.

"May I?"

He gestured to the empty place beside him.

"Cigarette?"

"Don't use them." He remembered that the expression came from NATO radio and was probably inelegant. He added "Thank you," and glanced at the Professor—whose attention, however, was all on his cigarette and his lighter.

The Professor gave no sign of wanting to talk.

And would probably have been astonished to learn that the young man at his side had felt himself, for a brief but agonized and recent time, to be a doubleganger, a stranger, just arrived at Palazzo Rovigliano at the age of twenty, along with a birth certificate. Or rather a new-looking copy of a birth certificate, his own, that he had found one day lying under his textbooks on a table in the hall outside his bedroom. He had never seen it before. In retrospect, he saw how crudely Vispo had contrived the discovery. At the time, he had thought Melba must have forgotten the certificate and left it there: he wondered why she had had the copy made. It revealed little that he didn't already know, but he found the sight of it disquieting, and didn't tell her he had found it.

After a day or two he took it to a tutor in jurisprudence at the university, one of several teachers with whom he had recently talked about future studies. He asked what the certificate meant.

The first reading brought the comment "An oddity." The second: "In more than one respect." Finally: "At the date of your birth, your father was married."

"Married and separated for many years. His wife—widow—is still living. She is not my mother."

"This makes it clear that she is not. Your father has had his name put down as father, whereas your mother is 'unknown.' If you were to look in the register of the office where your birth was reported, you would undoubtedly find a declaration by your father that you were his son by a woman who preferred not to be named. In those days, before our family laws were liberalized, a signed statement by a father was necessary to constitute 'recognition' of a child born out of wedlock. And only when a father 'recognized' a child as being his was the father's name put on the certificate. However, in those days 'recognition' by a married parent of a child born out of wedlock was impossible without the signed and notarized permission of the other spouse. And on this certificate of yours someone has written 'Permission of wife never received.' Which means that although your father apparently wanted to 'recognize' you, he was never able to because his wife refused consent. His name shouldn't be on the certificate at all. Somehow he succeeded in having it put there; and apparently later a clerk, perhaps the very clerk he had bribed, added the note—which amounts to a cancellation. You would probably find the same notation in the register.

"The designation of your mother as 'unknown' is another oddity, or at least a great rarity. Many birth certificates of children born out of wedlock in those days say 'Father N.N.'—*non noto:* unknown. It usually meant that the father refused to 'recognize' the child as his, or that the mother didn't want him to. But one almost never sees 'Mother N.N.' In fact, how can a mother's name, or at least her identity, not be known except when an infant is left abandoned? And especially in a case like this, where the father's name is given. Obviously, the determination to protect your mother was very strong.

"The fact that the certificate is dated from Rovigliano itself might explain its irregularities. It's a very small town. Your father could probably make himself persuasive there: a strong feudal tradition often survives in such places. By the way, I assume you know you've always had a perfect right to the name Rovigliano, even if your parents weren't married? The law allows the name of a town to be given as a surname, if desired, in such circumstances. Your father probably knew that, and the provision fits the case nicely. Undoubtedly his ancestors—your ancestors—either took their name from the town, or gave it. Which came first is seldom certain. Is there no one to tell you who your mother was?"

"I can only say I've never succeeded in finding out."

As he said that, the first hollow feeling came, the onset of the worst of the trouble.

"Have you thought of asking in Rovigliano? There might be an old official or pensioner who remembers things."

And as Ladislao was leaving: "By the way, have you decided? You know we'd be happy to think you were preparing to come with us."

LOOKING BACK on his turmoil now, he saw it as a banality, a condition one was continually hearing about in others, called "nervous crisis." ("Brain fever," the old term, used in Via Lupo, was more expressive: there were moments when one's head seemed on fire.)

Everyone in his second-year class at the university was obliged to inscribe himself as preparing for one or another faculty. There was nothing binding about it: one could always change. Some of the students had long known what their paths would be; others found even pro-forma election intimidating. His own realization, as the inscription day approached, that he would be absolutely unable to declare a choice, was like an onset of paralysis; and it was accompanied by a medley of sensations—especially a strange and sinister glare that illuminated and transformed familiar things. The carcass of the old palazzo-tenement swarming with neighbors and rats; the isolation of his and Melba's existence in the midst of it all; Melba's confusions and obsessions. More than anything else, the Club, its presence hitherto accepted without much thought, loomed as a sordid malignancy; Melba's employment for the sake of his studies was a disgrace to himself. Professors, classmates, books—the world he had inhabited—suddenly lay on the opposite side of a chasm: there was no reality in choosing a path there. He broke off the affair he'd been having with an enchanting dark-haired studentessa, shunned his friends.

That was his state of mind when he came on the certificate. The sight of "Mother N.N." agitated him. Even though from earliest memory he had been aware of a protected mystery.

The bedtime story had never varied.

"Tell me about Mamma, Melba."

"You know it so well, darling. Duca married a beautiful American girl but they had no children. Then years later he met the perfect person and you were born, and I went and brought you home because it all had to be kept secret. Her name must never be known. It would be dangerous for her. A great scandal. It's all a lovely mystery."

He had heard it over and over again.

The answers to his why's and what's were just as constant. "Because God didn't send them any." "Because she wasn't supposed to have children, you see." "A scandal is . . ."

His early acceptance of the lovely mystery was complete; and it endured. Nothing could have been more ingrained. It had never been tantalizing.

That state of things eased other acceptances. When the man named Vispo arrived and rented the Club room, understanding of who he was seeped in like osmosis. The process was helped along by the older tenants of the palazzo, who in the courtyard often conveyed news to Don Ladì.

". . . and the Duca paid a family in Sardinia to adopt him and bring him up."

"It was the Principessa's idea. It was she who got his mother's consent. His mother was Concetta, out at the farm. She was paid something, too, of course. The Principessa told her it would give the boy a better life because he was so clever, and you can see it did. He didn't come back even for Concetta's funeral. Now he's back for good, and we're supposed to call him Signore with his new family name, but sometimes we forget and just say Pasquale."

"He'd much rather we didn't forget."

"There's something else you can see he'd prefer different. Finding a certain young person here who's allowed to call himself Rovigliano."

"Me? I am a Rovigliano!"

"So is he. But he had to go away and become a Vispo. You didn't."

"Of course I didn't."

No trauma there. And everything went smoothly with Signor Vispo.

Once in a while the old tenants touched on the "lovely mystery" itself.

"The year you were born the Principessa went away. She stayed away quite a while, and when she came back she had you with her."

"You're the absolute image of her."

"She thinks of herself as your mother."

"Why shouldn't she?"

No trauma there either. Because Melba constantly did speak like a mother—she always had so spoken. "Go to sleep, my baby." With a smile to a quizzing young visitor: "Who's Ladi's mother? Why, what do you think I am? Of course I'm his aunt. But I can be his mother too, can't I?" "What a splendid school report! No mother was ever so proud of her son."

He thought of all that on the way to Rovigliano, the crazy idea gaining ground as the train carried him forward. Then a bus, and—the seat of his remote ancestors, previously unvisited though so near. Never was a little southern town more dreary and dusty, more meridional. Empty of any allure to mask revelations he might have cause to dread. At the registry office in the city hall a slatternly girl made eyes at him, gave him a wink when she saw the certificate with its N.N. She produced the register, and it was as the university jurist had said.

"I'd like to talk with a person who might know about this. Is there someone who was here at the time?"

"At the time! Twenty years!" She seemed indignant. She opened a connecting door and called, bringing forth a pinch-faced clerk wearing paper cuffs. No, there was no one left from that time, no no no, Signore.

"I don't mean in this office. In the town. Someone who might recall . . ."

"No no no. Nobody." He looked at the register and certificate. "But this is a copy that was made recently. Who are you, Signore?"

Once again Ladislao produced the identification the girl had required.

"But the other person. The one who came for this copy. His identification must have been in order; otherwise we wouldn't have given it to him. We are very particular." He addressed the girl. "You remember? The nasone . . ."

Not Melba, as he had been supposing. A nasone—a man with a long nose.

The girl whispered something.

"Yes, that was it." The clerk summoned the resentful tremor which, in bureaucrats, passes for defiance. "A permit from the Ministry."

Ladislao saw that as the subject of previous inquiry by a privileged investigator he merited only suspicion in this office: there would be no respect or help. As he walked away, hostility was hot on his back.

How had Vispo done it? Did "permit from the Ministry" mean a cash bribe to the clerk? Or had Vispo really obtained a ministerial permit? If the latter, perhaps Melba herself, on one of her trips to Rome for the Club, had picked it up, ignorant as usual of what her errand was. But this was not Club business. A personal—face it, a family—affair. *Why* had Vispo done it? Had he decided, after years of quiet, to unsettle the "certain young person who was allowed to call himself Rovigliano"? If so, this first move had been an experiment, to see whether a reminder of details might produce an effect.

Then chance had entered in. Vispo could scarcely have known how well he had chosen his moment. Under the circumstances, the sight of the N.N. had evoked old hints by the tenants; and some fearful days had been filled with a new interpretation of Melba's bedtime stories. After the visit to Rovigliano he had wallowed in sludge. Had enlisted in the Club, almost welcomed the sordid assignments. That might have been mere sudden compulsion to ease Melba's burden; but he knew it was not. It was a real fit. Then the fit blew itself out.

However, following Vispo's undisguised glee in the humiliation there were signs that the campaign was still on, and along much the same lines. The Club member delegated to escort him from the jail to Swank had said, "Your mother is coming to the island tomorrow"—said it casually, as though in the Club the parentage was taken for granted. He had answered, "You mean my aunt"; but at Swank today he had heard the manager tell the Americans the same story: "The son of a principessa."

He could cope with that tactic now. It had lost its force; he was sure it was nonsense. But he suspected that other gambits would be tried.

And now something else had come, from another direction. The Professor's news about the silence at Salerno. He knew that the recent fit had left him sensitive, easy prey to morbid imaginings and returns of the hollow feeling. But if Melba had been silent about him, that was no fantasma: it was as real as Vispo's moves. Was it a confirmation of feelings of his own? Uncertainty about Melba had been preying on his mind. He had long been familiar with her vagaries. But that they might include reservations about *him* was a possibility he had previously been blind to. All his life she had been his affectionate mother. But . . . Was he fancying it, or had her concern for him come to sound a little—mechanical? Perhaps the struggle was simply too prolonged, the course too hard; but lately the flat seemed full of her effort, her duty, her responsibility—all for him. It had never occurred to him to question his place in her life—or her heart. That she should leave him unmentioned during hours of prattle to—of all people—this . . . this family historian, one could almost call him, gave him a chill sensation of solitude.

BESIDE HIM, the cigarette that had been smoked in silence was finished, the stub ground into the earth.

"Professor . . ."

"Not Professor. I haven't been one for years."

"Signore—Sir—when you saw my aunt in Salerno—when was it?"

"Thursday. Last Thursday. She was just returning to Naples."

Thursday night. The bar pantry of the Imperatore. Voices coming through the partition, with a crescendo each time the slide went up to let through another tray of dirty glasses. Such a clatter that he didn't hear Carlo the waiter come in, and was startled by the rough grasp on his shoulder. "Telefono!" He went out in his grubby apron. As he made his way among the guests he saw that to them he *was* an apron—to the lovely girls and young women (he might well have happened to know some of them) laughing and chatting with family or friends. Of course Signor Mario and the others in their smart white jackets looked disgusted. Vispo said: "At first they refused absolutely to call you to the phone. When I put on the pressure they changed their minds. Here's somebody wants a word." And Melba: "I felt a need for reassurance."

Why, now, had the Professor come and sat silently beside him? Was he thinking of his embarrassment on realizing that the mother of twenty-year-old Ladislao Deming Rovigliano couldn't possibly be the legitimate Duchess?

The Professor was speaking. "Ladislao—if you'll allow me to call you that—you know I'm what might be called a friend of several generations of your family."

Why should his eyes smart as he heard this man call him by his first name? A name so charged with the ancestry Melba constantly talked about that he sometimes hated it. "Yes, I know that."

"So perhaps you'll forgive me for asking . . ."

Was a question about his mother coming now?

"Why is your aunt in this sordid place? With all these bestial people? And why are *you* here?"

He rubbed his stinging eyes. When, ever, apart from teachers' compliments, had an older man spoken to him like this?

Once again, as in the Imperatore pantry, he felt a heavy hand on his shoulder. The manager. "I called. You weren't paying attention. Come along. Change of plan."

25

"O SIGNORA!"

Melba heard the Swank ferryman call after her as she was leaving the pier on her way to the funicular and the convent. "There's Reverend Mother now—there, by the Customs House."

On the quay a black-gowned, white-coiffed figure was approaching a building flying the Italian tricolor. Melba saw the nun go through the door, but by the time she herself reached the entrance hall it was empty except for a young clerk at a desk. His radio played softly beside him.

"Yes, Signora?"

"I saw a friend of mine come in here just now. I was hoping to have a word with her."

"Madre Serafina? She's inside, conferring with the Maresciallo."

Conferring! The Maresciallo was no mere customs inspector: a revenue officer, into whose presence privilege alone could have granted such rapid admission. "May I wait?"

"Imagine, Signora! A friend of Reverend Mother need ask no such permission. No, no; not that chair. Something more comfortable. This one, Signora. Make yourself comfortable here, Signora."

The two chairs were identical. But from her "more comfortable" one Melba was soon aware that the other was closer to a door through which came the sound of voices—voices badly blurred by the time they reached her. "Forgive me," she murmured. "I think I prefer that chair after all": and making the move with Sacred Heart grace, she was in it.

The clerk touched his radio; a raucous voice filled the air. But how could he know that one had been trained by a jukebox to concentrate below the level of a music barrage?

"... patient for a week ... nothing coming in ... now I hear ..."

"Alas, Reverend Mother ... radically changed situation ... the Consortium ..."

"... meeting this morning ... outrage ... all my scrupulous fairness with you, Maresciallo ... never failed to share ... base ingratitude ... your duty to protect us poor ..."

"Alas ... helpless, Reverend Mother ... desolated ... I myself ... losing your inestimable generosity ..."

"... carry this matter to Rome!"

"... alas, Reverend Mother! ..."

Fragments, but not unsuggestive. Rising shrillness. (The radio voice rose also). In reply, murmurs of impotence and distress.

And then, after a silence, the sound of chairs pushed back.

The door opened.

Two colorless visages. Differently so. The wrinkled parchment of the nun, one could see, was her natural complexion: it was in the dark eyes that the emotion of the moment burned, and anger had compressed the pale lips to invisibility. Whereas the strained pallor of the man in uniform, a victim, reviled even while suffering cuts in his income, was the particular, distressing transformation of a skin usually lustrous. His thick black moustache seemed to be flourishing on a corpse.

Melba rose. "Reverend Mother ..."

The nun's intention to leave the Customs House directly was manifest: pause or further speech was not in her program. But a glance at Melba stopped her. The two women stood, peering into each other's eyes.

Melba was seeking what she had last seen in this face twenty years before; and she supposed the nun was doing the same. Gradually, slowly, from under or behind the ashen mask sharply framed by the coif there emerged the features, always pale, always severe, but in those days handsome and sensual, of the young island woman, her hair as dark as her eyes, who had come to work in the Neapolitan tobacco shop in Via Lupo. And, having discovered her, Melba did not lose her, but continued to see her as she had been.

And to what depth, she wondered, did the other have to penetrate to see the old—that is, the younger—Melba? For what seemed many moments the nun continued silently to peer. Surely there was not that much change. Professor Haley had recognized her instantly on the street in Salerno. She wore no disguising coif and veil. And just yesterday her hair had been made its most becoming by the best coiffeur in Naples. Still the nun stared. And Melba knew why. What was keeping the other fixed and wordless in this surprise encounter was not lack of recognition, but reflection—or, to use a word that had always fitted the case, calculation. Calculating what to say and how to say it.

"Here I am,"—Melba herself decided to say—"Reverend Mother."

The Maresciallo and his clerk were watching and listening. The radio was a mere murmur.

The nun said coldly: "Have you a card?"

For the second time in less than a week Melba produced from her handbag a bit of crested pasteboard. Not Terry's card this time, but her own. Simpler: "Millicent Rovigliano," with just the ducal coronet to tell that part of the story. With Fedora there was every reason to be herself.

Taken and examined, the card disappeared inside the nun's wide sleeve. The frigidity did not diminish. "I am busy, Signora. Immensely busy. Immensely preoccupied."

"It is precisely the subject preoccupying you, Reverend Mother, that I have come to discuss."

"And precisely what subject is that, pray, Signora?"

Melba glanced at the two staring men and back to the nun.

Fedora Sacca was mistaken if she thought she could force her to speak her lines before an audience, even an audience of two. Especially—and this was for Fedora's own benefit—when the audience included an official who might well expect, on hearing Melba's message, to benefit again from Fedora's "inestimable generosity." But her mute appeal for privacy was ignored. Neither nun nor men made a move; and she could think of nothing better to do than to lean forward and murmur a single word into a coif-covered ear. That brought result. It also impressed on Melba another difference wrought by twenty years. That Fedora Sacca should demand a reason before consenting to talk with a Rovigliano . . .

The nun made a motion of the head, a peasant or proletarian motion signifying "Come"; and oblivious of the two officials the women left the Customs House and were soon walking along the quay toward the funicular.

MELBA ASSUMED that there would be silence between them until they reached their destination; and so there was, as the car bore them slowly upward, as they crossed the piazza, passed before the church, and entered the ancient building beside it. During the journey, especially in the funicular, alone with her in a compartment, the nun all but devoured her with stares of appraisal and curiosity; and inside the convent, where she was led down a corridor straight into what was indubitably a parlor, furnished with a set of nineteenth-century chairs upholstered in red plush, Melba reflected that were her errand anything but what it was, she might well feel herself very much the fly.

"CAFFÈ!" The order was given to no one in particular—it was simply barked loudly out. That was Victorian, too, like the furniture—reminiscent of the great Queen's aplomb at the Opéra, when she impressed the Parisians by sinking into her chair without glancing to be sure it was being held. After the bark, silence returned, and was weirdly maintained. Melba had resolved not to speak until spoken to, and she held to the resolve, only smiling now and again in reply to a look that was particularly piercing. Finally there was a knock on the door: a young nun entered and placed on a table a silver tray bearing cups and sugar. When she had retired, one of the cups was silently offered. Melba took. She sipped. There was a moment's astonished pause, and pure delight made her break her vow. *"Scaticchio!"*

"Ah, Signora, you recognize?!"

"Ah! How not?"

It would have taken a deadened palate not to recognize the delicious beverage. Where could it come from, if not the little coffee bar a hundred yards down Via Lupo from Palazzo Rovigliano that looked like nothing and served coffee unequaled in the world? Owned and run for a hundred years by the family whose name it bore; adored by generations of Neapolitans; its product unmistakable.

"But how here, Reverend Mother?"

The answering voice was gruff, but the words hinted at détente. "Our coffee-sister, Sister Silena—not the one who *served* the coffee; that was a servant-sister; we have two kinds here—was a Scaticchio. The worldly bustle of the bar . . ."

"Bustle" was the word. The heavenly Scaticchio espresso drew crowds from dawn to midnight. Melba herself, when out on errands, seldom renounced the luxury.

". . . became wearisome to her, and she joined our Community. The family recipe was part of her dowry." Melba may have imagined it, but following the word "dowry," was there a hesitation, a glance, quickly withdrawn? "We operate, here in this convent, what you might call Scaticchio's only branch. You saw it as we came in, Signora."

The booth in the corner of the cloister just inside the entrance? Workmen had been standing in front of it: Melba had assumed it to be a porteress's lodge.

"Our little coffee bar is an island institution. It is open to the public from matins to vespers. On the basis of voluntary contributions, as we are of course unlicensed. It brings us some slight revenue. When one's Parroco is a thief, as ours is, one does what one can to be self-supporting. Several of our sisters practice specialties. Wait: I will call Sister Silena."

"SILENA!" The name, not lending itself to a bark like "CAFFÈ!", was nonetheless powerfully bellowed. And the young nun who almost immediately appeared, after curtsying, just inside the door, to the Reverend Mother, glanced at Melba, cried *"Principessa!"* and rushed over with outstretched arms.

"You SEEM to have become the very godmother of Via Lupo, Signora!" The Reverend Mother knew how to make her point. "In my day you knew us all, of course, but there was less ... familiarity. Is it a sign of the times?"

The felinity, the persistent absence of "Principessa," did not go unnoticed by Melba. But again she merely smiled. She had no intention of recounting to Fedora Sacca the changes in her life that had made it perfectly natural for the former little Carmelina Scaticchio, overcome by memories of the old neighborhood, to babble happily until a few words from the Reverend Mother, gently enough delivered for once, had sent her back, beaming, toward her coffee bar. They had even kissed.

The coffee-maker's recognition had put an end to the spurious probation—the form Fedora had given to the delay she had apparently needed while deciding on her own comportment. There was no apology for the absurd identity tests. Business began. "You accosted me for a particular purpose, Signora. Will you tell me what it is?"

"Could the door be shut all the way, Reverend Mother? And kept shut?"

As before, the order was bawled to the invisible. The latch clicked.

Melba opened her large handbag and withdrew Signor

Vispo's package. She untied it, extracting one by one the packets of bank notes and laying them on the table. Several piles grew. The nun's face was impassive. The last bundle joined the others. Melba closed the bag. "From my employers, Reverend Mother. A lump compensation for loss of revenue. They hope you will find it generous."

The nun was slow to reply. She lifted and examined each bundle, rearranging the piles. Only when the counting was finished did she look up. "The new supplier? The so-called Consortium?"

Melba nodded.

"Then I do not understand. The Maresciallo . . . Just now he was sobbing because he had been definitely told he could expect nothing."

Vispo had armed her with the answer to that. "It is up to you whether the Maresciallo is to share, Reverend Mother. My employers prefer to contribute to those who really count, allowing them to decide whether something should trickle downward. In the context of my employers' many connections, the Maresciallo is an unimportant underling. They recognize that you are scarcely that."

"We are all His underlings, Signora."

Melba momentarily shut her eyes, to blot out the sight of the skyward-pointing finger. From the moment the tone had been chosen, she had been awaiting the first sign of overplay. No one could have had Fedora's career without overplay being a way of life. Now the pious gesture, admonitory, almost proprietary, did not interrupt the other hand in what had become its veritable caressing of the piles on the table. Then a key was chosen from a cluster hanging on a thong from the leather girdle, the table drawer was unlocked, the bank notes inserted, the lock turned. The nun rose. "Please tell your employers that I accept my—*tip.*"

A scimitar of a smile followed the word. Rough give and rough take were in the Club's line of work: Melba could imagine Signor Vispo relishing Fedora's form of thanks; indeed it was easy to see Fedora herself as a Club member, doing jobs that she,

Melba, was unfit for. During this half hour the nun had become quite recognizable as the tobacco-shop Fedora plus twenty years of having her own way. All bridges burned; no curiosity expressed about anyone or anything except as to the immediate reason for this visit. A remarkable performance! Only Melba, probably, in all the world, since Riccardo was dead—and poor Riccardo had never been noted for perception—would have recognized what lay behind those identity tests: what had made them, or some other delaying tactic, essential even for Fedora. Even Fedora must be plagued by an occasional dream.

As the Reverend Mother rose, Melba's crested card fluttered from her black sleeve onto the table. She retrieved it, and as though in response to a message communicated by her thumb, which passed several times over the surface, she took it up, examined it, and for a moment glanced speculatively at Melba. "Come with me, Signora. We'll make a little detour on your way out."

Undisguised though it was, the dismissal was less brusque than Melba had been prepared for.

They left the parlor. Halfway down the cloister—where Carmelina Scaticchio waved over a hedge of customers—Fedora opened a door in a wall and led Melba through. Immediately they were standing inside the church—large, lofty, and domed.

"Enemy territory, Signora!"

Melba, who had crossed herself on discovering where she was, quickly did so again to purge the enormity she had to believe she had heard. Among all the nuns of the world, was there another capable of being driven by circumstances so to refer to the house of God?

"I have sometimes been tempted to lock that door from our side. But to do so would harm our case. Because our point, in our complaint against our thieving priest, is the fact of the old monastery, and hence our present community, being an integral part of the church. Come this way."

Down a side aisle, near the altar crossing, the Superior stopped before a chapel housing an elaborate funerary monument. Lying on a sarcophagus, beneath an escutcheoned canopy held by a pair of floating angels—all in carved stone—a life-size stone effigy in ruff and doublet was half-recumbent, his moustachioed head, resembling Shakespeare's, resting on an upraised forearm and hand. Between elbow and chest he was cradling the model of an ecclesiastical building. Cut into the marble base supporting the whole was a long Latin legend, out of whose chiseled, black-painted letters there loomed, in large red capitals, the name SACCA.

The nun pointed to the chapel floor, paved with black and white marble slabs. "I think you never met my ancestors, Signora. Most of them are down there, in the family vault. You recognize the building the one on the tomb is holding? This very church, restored as the inscription says by his munificence. Munificence! On an island this size the wherewithal for munificence doesn't survive testamentary divisions over countless generations. We Saccas of today have to fend for ourselves, like everybody else. We have to forget all that."

"That" was illustrated by another gesture: the nun reached out and touched with a forefinger the word immediately following SACCA: "BARONE." But Melba, as she followed the finger, saw those letters as though blurred, dissolving into the import of the whole. For what she had just heard differed astonishingly from the impersonality of everything said in the parlor. It constituted a veritable autobiography—a "Do you remember?" Who had "fended" for herself if not Fedora? And although Riccardo had never stinted himself in his appetite for coarse girls, he would never have chosen this one from the tobacco shop for his particular purpose had he not assured himself, by a visit to her island—it must have been to this very tombside—that what she had told him about her family was true. "Good blood" had been essential, since the entire purpose was inheritance. No matter if its bearers had over the centuries become indistinguishable from the rest of the local populace, very small bourgeois if not near-peasants. For Riccardo, that made it easier; even, probably, possible.

To the other women, when they had become mothers of his children, there had been payments. That was the usual practice; mere decency. But among the memorable differences between them and Fedora had been Fedora's cool pointing out that the entire dowry must be paid in advance, because she had no reason to trust Riccardo's word should, through no fault of her own, "things not take," as she put it, or the result be a girl. In fact the gamble element, appealing to another of Riccardo's ruinous traits, was perhaps what had clinched the matter, making it irresistible.

And here today, Fedora, reigning in her convent, just as coolly accepting another payment from the hands of a Rovigliano— a Rovigliano reduced to an occupation that was squalid if not criminal—was reminding her of all that by pointing out that she, too, if she wished, could have a crested bit of pasteboard.

Nor did she stop there.

"The poem says it happened the same way to a lot of us in this part of the country, Signora. In fact, on the same day. You know it, I suppose."

"The poem?"

"The poem about the Holy Roman Emperor on a visit to southern Italy. The time a lot of rowdy petitioners woke him up at the castle where he was spending the night. You don't know it? Here on the island we all learned it as children. I often recited it to . . . to your brother. The Emperor comes out on a balcony in his nightshirt. It goes:

"Barons! Your Highnesses! For such you must be,
"Presuming to wake me before it's struck three!
"Raising a racket when it's not even dawn!
"Your Emperor, Barons, commands you be gone;
"And if before noon he should hear one more sound
"He has plenty of troops here to quickly surround

"The whole stinking lot of you, all—do you hear?
"And then—off with your heads! Clear the ground—disappear!"
Now out from the barracks the Emperor's troops rush,
And the rustics slink off amidst a great hush.
But those bumpkins remembered the Emperor's word,
Scornfully uttered, yet solemnly heard:
" '*Baroni*' he called us! And *Baroni* we'll stay!"
And every descendant's a Baron today.

The nun recited the doggerel as she must have done in childhood, keeping her eyes rolled upward while she spoke, as though reading the words in the air. Much was in local dialect; the rustic accent into which she fell grew steadily stronger; the last couplet rang out in earthy exultation. Then, with scarcely a pause, she added in her normal voice: "Your brother loved that. He thought it probably did happen that way. In some small town. Maybe Rovigliano itself. Who knows? Much more likely than the story about being descended from King Ladislao. Baroni, duchi, principesse—what's the difference? You and I would probably find we're cousins, if we looked back far enough. Today most of us are in the same boat, aren't we? I noticed your card was printed, not engraved."

Probably only what happened next could have kept Melba from making some answer she would later have regretted. Whether it would have taken the form of helpless indignant splutter, or whether she could have sufficiently mastered herself to utter poised words establishing distinctions, she was never to know. Pandemonium spared her. Suddenly, overhead, there broke out a pealing of bells that filled the church with unreal cacophony. Then the sound changed, to resemble that of an organ. Next, clangor merged with insidious melody; and finally all turned into supersong, rendered by what must originally, long ago, before it was processed, have been a human soprano voice, now issuing from the lungs of an apparatus. The words themselves were blurred, and rumbled as they came down through the roof of the church; but Melba knew them well. How frequently she heard that very song, each time containing a different name, over NATO radio! "Today's birthday message is sung at the request of Colonel Henry Perkins.

> *Happy Birthday to you!*
> *Happy Birthday to you!*
> *Happy Birrrrrth-day, dear Gladys,*
> *Happy Birthday to you!*

Congratulations, Glad; that message came to you with the affectionate greetings of your loving husband, Hank. We hope you were as happy to hear it as we were to sing it. The weather forecast for Naples and vicinity is . . ."

That was the way it constantly came over the air.

And here, today, in the church, as though once were not enough, the cycle was repeated, the sound crashing relentlessly down from the vaulting.

> *Happy Birthday to you!* . . .

The nun's face was a storm cloud. She looked as her voice had sounded through the door in the Customs House. Melba saw her lips move, forming a comment on the electronics: the term she used, common in Via Lupo, was scarcely to be expected from a nun in church. Then she was speaking into Melba's ear: "What are they saying?"

Melba shouted. "It is in English."

"What are they *saying*, Signora?"

"They are wishing somebody happy birthday."

"Giulio? This time, didn't I hear the name Giulio?"

"I think so. Wait while I listen. Yes. They are wishing some Giulio happy birthday."

"*Giulio!* Signora, what time is it? What time?"

"It is three . . ."

"Come, Signora, come. *Come!*"

A rush to the door, through the door, along the cloister. *"Anagrafe!"* Melba thought she heard shouted back to her, as she followed the flying habit. "The anagrafe will soon be closing!" The anagrafe was the local registry office, repository of vital statistics concerning island residents. "Wait for me here, Signora!" There was the wave of a hand toward the door of the parlor; the flying figure hurried on. *"Telephone!"* it cried. *"Telephone the anagrafe!"*

Then there was silence, deep after the din.

Melba waited. Ten minutes, perhaps. Alone in the parlor. Silence everywhere. And then the sound of approaching footsteps. The door opened. The Reverend Mother walked in—bringing with her, concentrated in her, all the quiet that pervaded the convent. Her face was paper-white. She let herself down into a chair. "I have him, I think." Her voice was low. "Thanks to you, Principessa, and your telling me the words, I think I have the Parroco." From her chair she slid to her knees on the floor. Her lips moved in silent prayer.

Melba shuddered.

26

YOUNG PADRE GIULIO, the Parroco, was puzzled by the antipathy which a number of islanders and visitors felt toward the carillon, and distressed by the sniggering that greeted some of his selections.

He had been assigned to the island parish by the Archbishop, who shared his modern views. It was typical of Giulio that he should several times have put it that way, rather than vice versa, when speaking with the Archbishop himself: "I am so glad, Your Excellency, that you share my views." Fortunately, the Archbishop was willing to tolerate, up to a certain point, the manners of the junior element among his seminarians—the younger professors, and recent students like Giulio, equally dedicated to the Church's modern way. Most of them came from families unacquainted with the niceties, and usually they lacked humor, imagination and tact. He believed that the arrogance resulting from those very defects strengthened their ability to deal with the doltish majority of the faithful. Occasionally one of them became too self-assertive, and the Archbishop brought him down. Not physically: but a bringing-down by the Archbishop had been known to reduce more than one brawny ordained peasant to tears and spasms. Antagonizing the Archbishop was best avoided.

A year or so before, the Vatican had abolished several dozen saints—that is, stricken from the Church calendar the names of sundry legendary characters long called Saint This or Saint That, whose historical existence modern scholarship found improbable. Among these was the patron saint of the island, a Neptune-like figure inherited from pagan mythology and reputed to protect sailors and fishermen against danger at sea. One of Giulio's first acts as Parroco had been to cancel the chief local religious festival— the centuries-old annual celebration in the ex-saint's honor: High Mass, the pelting of his image with flower petals and fish-heads as it was carried in procession with brass band, singing, and the chanting of litanies; and, at night, fireworks, feasting and dancing. Giulio had expected, and willingly endured, his resultant un-popularity. He hoped to reduce it, with time. But unpopularity was a small price to pay for the privilege of upholding the Church's modern line: emphasis on the direct worship of God; concentration on Him, as opposed to the old dispersal of prayers and attention to saints and other interlopers both living and dead.

The island church which he had been given to administer, Giulio considered His—God's—local home. His alone. That is, *almost* no one else's. (At the seminary it was often rumored that "even the Madonna is on her way out"—a position not yet taken publicly.) It was certainly not the home of nuns. They had their own home, next door. As Parroco, Giulio was maintained by the diocesan office, not by the parishioners. Parishioners' offerings were made specifically to Him. To share them with the occupants of the former monastery had been merely a tradition: there was no obligation under Church or civil law. The nuns merited a small recompense for garnishing the altar, laundering its napery, and performing a few other household chores: but no more. Keeping the roof of His house in repair outweighed the tradition to which they appealed. If the Mother House of their order, wherever it was, did not support them adequately, that was their affair. Giulio knew of Madre Serafina's trafficking in salt. He knew about the coffee bar in the cloister. He even knew that one of the sisters, an expert trousers-maker, was kept busy during the tourist season measuring and fitting not only women, but men, for the bell-bottomed slacks now fashionable. In tolerating such activities as those, surely he deserved if not the nuns' gratitude, at least their courtesy.

As to the cassettes, he could read some English, and understood pretty much what the words said. It was this understanding which caused part of his puzzlement: it seemed to him that the cassettes' expression of spiritual feeling was in the right idiom for today's listeners. Many of the songs he had chosen came close to being prayers. Take "You're the Top": what was that if not a laudamus? Or another of his favorites:

> *You'd be so easy to love,*
> *So easy to idolize*
> *All others above. . . .*

Who could possibly object to that? Old-fashioned though the islanders fundamentally were, they had adopted many elements of the modern—the American—way of life: every family had its television, and the young were passionate for rock music, pinball machines, and bubble gum. Surely "Easy to Love" was more elevated than bubble gum?

It was not true that he had bought the installation. That was a lie maliciously spread by the nuns—by the Reverend Mother, who certainly knew better—and persistently "believed" by many parishioners, though he had several times announced the gift from the altar and even named the donor.

He had welcomed the munificence of the rich Italo-American, president of an enormous music corporation, who had come to the island one summer, fallen in love with it from the Imperatore's poolside and bars, and offered its church this splendid embellishment. Giulio was enchanted by the sound of the carillon. He found it impossible to understand anyone's not finding splendor in its rich tones, so gloriously superior to the clanging of the old church bells and the braying of the local brass band.

In short, Giulio was precisely the wrong kind of Parroco to have been sent to an island where, despite inroads of vulgarity, the pleasure-loving inhabitants, never completely converted from pagan ways, had retained much of their old simplicity, their instinct for what was seemly and what was not.

Unwittingly, he was beginning to pay for the Archbishop's mistake that early afternoon when the two ladies in his church— their presence unknown to him—were half-deafened by the mighty outpourings from the loudspeakers on the roof. However, as he inserted and twice activated that particular cassette, Giulio was not a completely happy man.

For the past few days, he had uncharacteristically recognized the existence of a dilemma.

Along with a few of the latest commercial releases, the donor had recently sent him this new cassette, a very short one, and a letter. A great and good friend of his, a famous, important man of whom Padre Giulio had undoubtedly heard—and he named him— would soon be arriving at the island on his yacht. At least, his wife would. Padre Giulio could make a very gracious gesture. It was probable that the days of the yacht's presence in island waters would include the great man's wife's birthday: he gave the date. She was a famous lady in her own right—he gave her name: Padre Giulio had probably heard of her, as well. On her birthday, would he please play this particular cassette? Play it several times, at different hours during the day, so that it would surely be heard on the yacht? The donor freely confessed that he was obligated to the great man for many favors: if the cassette could be played on that day, it would make everybody happy. Including, he was sure, Padre Giulio himself: for the great man and his wife were devout Catholics, wealthy and generous beyond imagining.

After reading the letter, Giulio played the cassette with the loudspeakers carefully turned off. He had heard of the couple: who had not? For the lady he had much sympathy. She was someone who had suffered immensely, a noble soul, worshipped by her countrymen, it was said—indeed by all the world.

Even so, to play what was a tribute to her, rather than to Him . . .

On the other hand, had he the right to obstruct benefits that might accrue to His house? The dilemma was still with him when the morning of the day came. It took him until early afternoon to decide.

The anglicized way the lady's name was spelled in the typed title of the cassette, HAPPY BIRTHDAY DEAR JULIA, made him think not at all of his own name. Despite his almost Papal sense of infallibility in religious matters, he was forgetful of his own person—the opposite of vainglorious. His own birthday? Year after year the date passed unremembered, unnoticed.

Looking out his study window, he saw that the huge gray vessel had reached the harbor.

He flicked the switch.

27

B<small>ECAUSE</small> of the unexpected camaraderie between the leathermen and those other Americans, Vispo saw that place of delivery
had to be changed.

As previously planned, Swank was to have been the sole
scene. After approval of sample and payment of confidence-giving
deposit, full delivery of the blue-packaged merchandise was to
have been accepted at the manager's counter. Whereupon, balance
of payment was promptly to have been made—in the form of
surprise attack. Quiet, efficient punishment, by the assembled Club
members, of whatever Nessiemen had come with the goods. That
was what the Consortium's chiefs had traveled from Rome to
enjoy.

Vispo looked on the whole *Nessie* affair as little more than a
joke anyway. No importance could be attached to a bit of amateur
smuggling by the crew of an American pleasure yacht, except
insofar as its punishment might serve as a warning to others. In the
context of the Consortium's program, even the unscheduled little
Gattopardo II had been more significant, playing as it did a role,
however tiny, in the overall Sicilian operation.

But that American trio. Veterans of the battlefield. And their
wives! All of them belligerent on arrival. Distrustful of the natives.
Loud-mouthed. Full of martinis, or toonies. Not apt to remain
unaware, or inactive, if something began to happen to buddies
from the *Nessie*. Their presence ruled out the possibility of quiet
chastisement. And Vispo knew that a swarming, vulgar free-for-all
was not in the Consortium's style.

As Vispo thought out the new plan, it seemed good to him. The sudden need for change was a boon. A nudge. A reminder of his own strength. His recent step up was no small one—from odd-job man for hire with goon squad, to director of the Consortium's Naples Salt Committee. Naturally he had been aware from the outset of the enormous increase in private opportunities. Fringe benefits, one might say. Already he had put one or two of them to good use. And now new forms of personal fulfillment suggested themselves.

So the manager was summoned to the bamboo bar and given instructions. On his way back to his office he relayed them quietly to the members in their deck chairs.

When the two leathermen finally finished drinking with the sextet and approached the counter with their blue bundle, and the older, shambling and uncouth, opened negotiations by mumbling "You know about this?," the manager nodded and asked to see the contents.

Quality, on examination, was pronounced good, and inquiry was made as to available quantity. When told that delivery should be made not to Swank, but "elsewhere," and that a guide would be furnished them, the leathermen reacted with distrust, which persisted even while the manager assembled the deposit in dollars. Only when he revealed the name of the actual buyer and described the delivery spot were the Nessiemen calmed. The manager then summoned the chosen guide.

The boy failed to respond, being deep in conversation with the American Professor, and the manager walked over to him. That was when Ladislao felt the hand on his shoulder and heard the words "Change of plan."

PART THREE

28

A FEW MINUTES after the Club had been alerted to the change of plan, Harry the choker walked over to Nat and Lyle and asked if they wouldn't like to "join us and the girls on a mini-cruise to the harbor." The *Nessie* was going there, it seemed, and their pals had offered them a lift. "Plenty of room for two more. From the harbor we know about getting to the hotel. Down at the dock in ten minutes if you're on."

Nat had no wish to be on, having just witnessed the fate of another yacht that had disgorged a package wrapped in that same conspicuous shade of blue. During the few days since Immac-olatina had replenished his cupboard—with an air of mystery, it was true, but with perfect calm—blue packages, synonymous with salt, had assumed a sinister aspect. Besides, unattractive though almost everyone at Swank was, he was for some reason loath to leave the place.

Lyle's ambivalence filled the interval allowed for decision. He longed to see his cousin's floating monster; but finally: "No, I'd much better not. Especially since I know she's not on board. She'd hear I'd been there, and be prepared to run into me. I have to take her by surprise. I can't afford to risk her just passing me by with her nose in the air."

Young Rovigliano approached them. He addressed Nat only, across a non-existent Lyle. "You're not coming, Professor? We're ready."

"We? You're going to the *Nessie* too?"

"I'm the guide, Professor."

"The guide for the Americans? To their hotel?"

"No. For the *Nessie* people. To the buyer."

"I'm coming."

THE LOAD OF eleven by no means filled the dinghy. Nat recalled flash-spotted magazine photographs of summer-night crowds on the café-lined waterfronts of Cannes, Portofino, Saint-Tropez, watching the Kaloumians and their guests disembark from this same craft. And contemplating the looming mass of the *Nessie* itself—it was unquestionably an "it," not a "she"—he thought that with its flattened funnel and slab-like stern the parent ship seemed to have been designed to harmonize with its most frequent companions in today's sea-lanes—the tankers: symbols of one segment of the Kaloumian empire.

When they had climbed the *Nessie*'s outboard ladder, the leathermen turned them over unceremoniously to a pair of unsmiling, white-jacketed stewards, who were standing in such readiness as to leave no doubt that they had been electronically alerted. These welcomers led the group off on what they announced as a guided tour of the ship. A euphemism, it soon turned out, for "guarded": like the leather jackets, these white ones bulged over the heart, and the next quarter hour was Indian file between gunmen. No lingering, it was plain; no branching off the path. The girls' twitterings—"Oh what a lovely treat!"—soon died away.

In contrast to the grim aspect of the *Nessie*'s hull, its interior was decorated in what one of the guides called "French Palatial," bringing to mind the lobbies and alcoves of many an old-style grand hotel. Conducted through First Salon, Second Salon, Picture Gallery, Cinema, Bar-Discotheque-Library, and Dining Saloon (the last in the course of being decorated with flora and foliage by stewards under the direction of a woman of secretarial aspect), they were several times told that "all the antiques were personally chosen by Mrs. Kaloumian herself"; and by the time they reached the Private Chapel it had become obvious that the tour was not so much sightseeing-with-surveillance as surveillance barely disguised as sightseeing. Probably this group was not more distrusted than any other, but in the eyes of the super-rich and their minions almost any visitors represent that unnerving element which is the rest of the world. Nat wondered whether even the Kaloumians' own guests, stellar and glittering though the magazines made them out to be, weren't sometimes made aware of the distinction.

Through an oak-paneled ogival door came a medley of sounds. Within, although the decor was appropriately ecclesiastic, the chapel was at that moment not a place of prayer and repose. A red-haired workman in overalls, standing on the altar and at first unaware of the party's entrance, was cursing in Cockney as he struggled to pry loose a large picture embedded in the wall. His pinch bar, encountering resistance, was rasping loudly. So far he had succeeded only in obscuring the face of the picture with plaster dust, and chips were raining down on the tabernacle and altar steps. The guards were just making an about-face, gesturing that this part of the visit was canceled, when the noise stopped and the workman called out. "Either of you lads know about this picture? Is it worth all this trouble, or can I just rip it out of the frame? Mrs. K. said it should be removed, but did she say it should be saved?"

The stewards exchanged glances and shrugs, but made no other answer. Silence fell. Nat became aware that Ladislao was staring at him, moving his head and eyes back and forth between him and the altar; he seemed to be urging him to step in and help. After a moment Nat spoke: "May I take a look?"

The stewards replied only with stolid glares. The atmosphere, heavy with "security," did not encourage an uninvited move. Nat waited. "I assume Rosencrantz and Guildenstern won't shoot you if you do," the workman finally said. With a sleeved arm he roughly dusted the picture's surface.

As all watched, Nat joined him on the altar.

The light was poor, the varnish on the canvas thick; even the dusted parts were dim. He distinguished a recumbent figure of indeterminate sex. Higher, a male figure bearing something that looked like a pitchfork. Satan? Almost certainly not: the iconography of that personage was very limited. He knew that the owner of the *Nessie* bore the name of the martyr whose executioners had turned him, presumably with pitchforks, as he roasted; but in pictorial representations of that saint pitchforks were usually less prominent than the gridiron on which the victim lay, and here no gridiron was visible. Whatever the altarpiece represented—and despite the murk, its quality was plainly no better than that of the daubs walled up in Melba's salotto—it could still be removed without being destroyed.

"Try scratching the surface of the surround, about here and here. If you find the heads of screws or bolts, all you'll need is a screwdriver. More likely bolts. Probably fastened to a metal framework sunk in the wall: that's what your pinch bar is hitting. At least, I know that devices of that kind are used in museums."

Murmuring something that sounded to Nat like "Old Mantuan! old Mantuan!" the workman made a gesture of enlightenment.

One of the guards saw it, nudged the other, and barked: "Okay, Jack, this way out."

Jack, Nat presumed, was himself, and there was no quarreling about it. By the time he had clambered down, the G.I. sextet was already shuffling out the door, the S.S. pair standing alert as they passed: one could imagine them wielding knouts, if necessary. Ladislao, who had hung back, was looking at Nat again, moving his head as before. There was no time to learn what his new or repeated message was: in a few moments everyone was out. The rear guard, as he closed the door, called back, in mock Colonel Blimp, "Carry on, Coopah." There was no telling whether that was the workman's name or his title.

The group, filing out onto the deck, saw that the *Nessie* was just outside the breakwater; and along with the sextet Nat was directed toward the ladder. Ladislao moved close and said quickly: "I'm not coming ashore till later. Where can I find you?"

"Ask at the Imperatore." That was intended to save time, to spare the need for street, number, and house name; but when the boy half-smiled and shook his head, Nat remembered about him and the hotel. Ladislao then repeated after him the address of Villa Bklyn; and Nat followed the others down the gangway.

Sitting in the dinghy, he let his thoughts dwell on the prospect of seeing the boy again; and he was just becoming aware that this was his first pleasant expectation in many months when suddenly the church carillon broke the silence with something utterly familiar but new in the repertory. Following preludes by bells and organ, a brass-lunged soprano from another planet burst into song. The sextet in the dinghy, after shouts of surprise, joined lustily in, and their substituting of each other's names for that of the birthday person prevented Nat each time (the number was played twice) from hearing who was being electronically feted. Before the music, the Americans had been uncharacteristically quiet, apparently aware that the tour had been unsatisfactory; and their enthusiastic chorusing expressed relief at a return to the familiar after the yacht's strange atmosphere. Now their spirits rebounded, and by the time the dinghy reached the pier the girls were telling each other and Nat that the mini-cruise had really been "a wonderful and rewarding experience," and bidding an effusively grateful farewell to the black-leather helmsman. After all, they too had been in Arcadia.

Nat led them to the funicular, and they went up together. Although they had repeatedly cursed the skipper of the *Gattopardo II* and taken satisfaction in his arrest, they now showed themselves crippled by the lack of even so unsatisfactory a courier. In the piazza they huddled together, baffled, grumbling that the hotel, which they had been told was nearby, was not immediately visible. Nothing for it but that Nat take them in hand, shepherd them down the short street to the very desk of the Imperatore, identify them as "the party the manager of Swank called about," ask the concierge to help them telephone Naples about lost passports, and finally see them bowed by a reception clerk into one of the lifts on their raucous way to their quiet rooms.

Yes, he promised, he would tell the Princess they had arrived, if and when he saw her.

29

HE DID RUN into Melba almost at once, as he was leaving the hotel and she approaching it followed by one of the island's porters laden with bundles. She accepted his invitation easily. She could accompany him straightaway; she had found everything the Americans wanted, and there was no need for her to go to their rooms.

Now, AFTER AN HOUR with her on his terrace at Villa Bklyn, he knew something more about her presence that day in Salerno and here on the island.

The fortuitous sinking of the *Gattopardo II* provided the third leg of the salt story: Melba's details about herself and the "Club" revealed the authorship of the explosions, and she made no secret of the origins of the man she called Vispo.

But the curiosity roused in him by blue packages, a curiosity he would later recognize as the first flicker of reviving interest in daily events—the beginning, possibly, of the end of mourning—had quickly taken second place. For those concerned, the salt story would doubtless continue to unfold, with picturesque repercussions; but his own drive to investigate was now directed at a more personal object: the weird omission from Melba's memoirs.

"Ladislao, Melba."

"Ladislao? Yes? What about him?"

Apparently he would still have to spell it out.

"Melba: that afternoon in Salerno, describing your present life, you didn't tell me he existed. Earlier today you introduced him as your nephew. And now again you say nothing about him. You can imagine I'm interested: a descendant of Jason Deming in a new generation."

She seemed astonished. "Oh, but Laddie did come up that afternoon. I remember distinctly saying I had things to tell you about my brother and your book. It was when I was leaving to take the bus."

"Yes, you did say that. But what did it have to do with Ladislao?"

"Oh . . . You didn't make the connection?"

"What connection should I have made?"

"Between my brother's reading your book and the things I had to tell you. What could they be, except about Laddie? I mean, since the result of my brother's reading your book *was* Laddie. Don't you really know you're responsible for Laddie? I mean, for his being here?"

SHE HERSELF really didn't know to what extent his look of bewilderment surprised her.

So much had been happening lately. She might be incapable of clear thinking. There was a sensation of looking at things through a film. With great effort she discerned the possibility that Nat had, in fact, known nothing whatever about Laddie; and that in Salerno she had acted on the assumption of his ignorance. The "connection" was one he couldn't possibly have made. She must try to keep that in mind. His delicacy—no: what she must have imagined was his delicacy—in not asking her about Laddie that afternoon had left her grateful. That dreadful afternoon when she was still trembling from having witnessed the extinction of a young life. At first she hadn't realized just who Nat was. And then, when she remembered, she had quailed at the thought of raising the question of Laddie with someone not seen for over twenty years and probably never to be seen again. So, at least, she now told herself. Americans always wanted to know everything. She remembered Nat's questioning years ago, when he was writing his book—because he "wanted to get things right." Well, he had finished his book—and with what results!

Today, feeling that she owed him an explanation for her distraction in Salerno, she had told him about the Club, her mission, and the young Sicilian. But since it turned out that she had been right, after all, in assuming his ignorance about Laddie, her story was not enough for him. Naturally he was pressing her. She had said just enough to bewilder him. Now she could think of no way to avoid saying more, and she said it.

NAT, AFTER WHAT now came out, wavered between accepting the disclosures as complete—or, at least, as sufficient—and suspecting that something essential remained to be told. One thing was sure: he had had no previous inkling of the story.

The Duca, he learned, who had scarcely read a book in half a century, opened *Jason Deming* the day it reached the palazzo: and from the subsequent course of events it appeared that the book had given him a tremendous, belated, explosive and quite naïve revelation of the world of the printed word.

It couldn't have been the sympathy the book expressed for the old collector, or the details it furnished of the Midwestern Educational Institution's squalid behavior, that roused him to take the steps he did. Family tradition had already acquainted him with the basic facts; he was already resentful. What occurred was the abrupt awakening of a pedigreed illiterate; his discovery, with an impact scarcely to be comprehended by habitual readers, that such things, things concerning him, matters of recent family history, could be found *in print, in a book.* And being *in a book,* they took on near-magic force.

Everyone had been astounded by his actions.

As though on fire, he rushed to his lawyers, brandishing *Jason Deming,* and ordered that letters be sent at once to the Institution, to the Duchess long repatriated in her midwestern American city, to the mayor of that city, to the governor of the state, if necessary to the President in the White House, demanding the instant return of the entire collection to its rightful owner—the basis for the demand being, quite simply, the actual presence of the facts of the case in a *book,* that very book he was holding in his hand. Surely the existence of the book must result in the return of the pictures. In short, although Melba didn't so put it, the apocalyptic discovery of the printed word had driven the poor Duca, never of the strongest intellect, quite mad. Mad, at least, on the subject of the lost collection.

When the lawyers, to humor him, wrote the letters, he raged at the mildness of their tone. He could scarcely believe the brevity and formality of the American replies. And when, to soothe him further, the lawyers warned that the attainment of his wishes might "take time," he turned cunning, resolving to defeat Time itself.

In Italy it had recently been announced that laws pertaining to the family were to be changed. "Recognition" of a child begotten or conceived out of wedlock by a partner in a marriage—bringing with it the child's right to inherit—would no longer require the consent of the parent's spouse. The Duca saw his opportunity. Since Vispo, his single already existing son (his other by-blows were girls), could not be envisaged as a successor, he would make a new, proper son and recognize him under the new dispensation. The Collegio Araldico, which ruled on the inheritance of titles, had its own strict requirements; but it was thought it would probably respect the new law to the extent of accepting, for the first time in its history, "recognized" offspring—*if* both parents were of proper ancestry. Thus, for the creation of a future Duca—an heir to carry on the fight for the pictures—a proper mother must be found.

"My brother found her. I knew her. I was present at the birth. I brought Laddie up. But things did not turn out as my brother had hoped. The passage of the new family law was blocked by the Church. My sister-in-law in America was written to, asked to consent to the recognition of this one child—naturally she had never been approached about the others. And naturally she refused. When he couldn't think of Laddie as his heir, my brother lost interest in him. During his last years his mind was clouded: much of the time he didn't know, let alone care, who the boy in the house with us was. He died just before the final passage of the new law, which would have allowed him to recognize Laddie. If what he did deserved punishment, he was amply punished, poor foolish Riccardo."

"Punished by dying mad, you mean, for having engendered a human life for so mad a purpose?"

"So mad a purpose? You think it mad, wanting to save the title? Now it's extinct. It would have been anyway, because the Collegio Araldico decided to continue to exclude 'recognized' children from inheriting titles."

"I meant something different. Thinking it would be possible to recover the pictures after a hundred years."

"The pictures! Now that they're being dispersed, what hope remains?"

Nat and Melba had learned, during their talk together, that they had both seen the story from the Great Lakes newspaper; and they were as one in excoriating the Institution.

There was a pause.

"Does Ladislao know who his mother is? Or was? At Swank the manager said 'the son of a principessa.' " There were so many principesse in Italy, true and false, well known and obscure. Which was Ladislao's mother?

Shaking her head, Melba repressed a smile. Naïve American!

In Italy, incest was part of history. She too had heard the manager, and knew that she herself was the principessa he meant. To Nat that was quite unthinkable. The fact that in this case Nat was right didn't make him the less innocent.

"Is there any reason he shouldn't know, at his age? Your not telling me about him in Salerno still mystifies me."

How unrelenting he was! If only she had stifled her cry at Swank, he might never have known that she and Ladislao were together.

"Oh, I might as well admit the truth—it was all Neapolitan superstition."

He probably remembered that the city abounded in such fancies. She couldn't pretend, being Neapolitan herself, to be immune to them. There were occasions when it seemed prudent to follow the tradition. The finger sign against the evil eye, for instance: so easily made, why not make it? Well, in Naples it was considered dangerous to mention the name of a loved one soon after someone resembling that loved one died. The meeting with Nat had come only a few hours after the death of the Sicilian boy. "He reminded me so much of Laddie!" Hence no mention of Laddie that day. She had been ashamed, she said, to confess this until now.

To which his only answer was: "I see."

Another pause.

Did he believe her? The story she had just invented was perfectly credible: it differed little from many an actual, traditional Neapolitan fancy.

Then he pressed her still further. He asked whether the work she and Ladislao were doing for Vispo wasn't dangerous.

"I think you mean 'dirty,' or 'disreputable,' don't you? I told you frankly the sort of thing I do for the Club. It's all I can do. Italian women of my generation and background weren't trained for work. As for Laddie . . . Once I saw an American television program about American boys doing what you call 'working their way through college.' Of course it showed only nice boys doing respectable kinds of work. Here we can't always choose. I wonder: don't you think that in America too there may be some even quite nice boys working their way through college not very nicely?"

Nat hadn't meant "dirty" or "disreputable." He had meant what he said: "dangerous."

He felt that he was struggling through a tangle—a tangle of some relevance and much obscurity. "Truth and fiction" might be putting it too crudely. What about "revelation and concealment"?

Just then someone rang the bell at the street gate.

30

AFTER THE DINGHY carried off the Professor and the others, Ladislao was able to slip back briefly into the *Nessie*'s chapel. Meanwhile, crewmen were bringing up blue packages from below deck; and when the dinghy returned they loaded it for redeparture. For this expedition two more leathermen joined the pair who had been at Swank. At the last minute the leader raised a finger to indicate that he had a thought. The others waited. The leader unbuckled his armpit holster and handed it to a steward. "Considering where we're going," he said. Ladislao, back on deck, watched the three other ceremonial unbucklings.

When they reached the island pier Ladislao's supervision began. Unloading into a taxi; and then, where motor traffic stopped at the edge of the village, reloading onto a porter's hand truck. During the short walk to the piazza the sight of the black-clad quartet created a noticeably sobering effect on passing citizens. On the doorstep of the building just beyond the church Ladislao told the others: "Better wait here."

Inside, a cloister, an espresso bar, a smiling nun at the machine.

"Reverend Mother, please?"

"What name shall I say?"

"She's expecting me. Just say Donna Millicent's nephew."

"Don Ladì! So grown up!"

For a moment he thought the vestal barmaid was going to kiss him. It was certainly in her mind to do so: she rushed out until she was close, then suddenly blushed and drew back. Perhaps she remembered her habit—or that he was no longer ten. "I'll get her for you, Don Ladì." Who was she?

A few minutes passed. All was quiet in the old convent.

"What makes you think I was expecting you?"

He was startled: the tall old nun—he had seen her before, striding about the village—had entered silently, and as he turned she was staring hard at him.

"You weren't expecting me, Madre? My aunt didn't say I was coming?"

"No." Still the stare.

Again unmentioned by Melba. But a moment's reflection told him that this time he was inventing disregard: Melba couldn't have announced him, for it was only after she left Swank to do her errands that Vispo had thought to give him this assignment, saying she would have been at the convent before him.

"Excuse me, Madre. These are the gentlemen I know you *are* expecting."

The leader of the gentlemen, impatient, had pushed open the street door and was peering at them.

Ladislao beckoned, and the four shambled in. After them, the porter hoisted his truck up the doorstep over the threshold. Ladislao announced: "The gentlemen from the yacht, Madre." And, turning to them: "Mother Serafina."

He did it gracefully: he had Melba's manner. In contrast, the mumble of self-introductions—"HickeyKellyO'ConnellO'Shanahan"—conveyed the abashment of mobsters in the presence of official spirituality.

Like a star in a well-directed scene, Madre Serafina stood tall over the spectacle before her. When she turned her eyes to the gentlemen and the packages, Ladislao thought her inspection of him was ended; but the sharp gaze kept returning, resting on him again and again. He bore it easily: he had no feeling of any kind for this old nun: she could stare all she liked. Being Neapolitan, he found her theatricality normal, but there did seem to be something inappropriate about her way of receiving this particular group of visitors, bearers as they were of business opportunity. She looked again at the packages, now a blue pile on the floor. "All that," she finally asked, "is for me?"

"That is the entire supply, Madre. You have been given precedence." He had been ordered to use those words.

"Very good. Then let's get it out of the way. Silena!" The coffee-sister came forward, was given an order, and disappeared.

Madre Serafina recognized a mix-up when she saw one. Coming after the confirmation by the Maresciallo that she would be offered absolutely nothing more, and after Donna Millicent's delivery of the Consortium's indemnity, what could this bonus be but a mix-up? Somebody's mistake. Not hers. Let it not lead to confusion or questioning. Not to ask where it came from or why this young man of all young men should have come with it. Simply accept. Another gift from God, the second today.

Led by Silena, a swarm of nuns swept into the cloister. Further orders were barked out. The black and white habits swirled like the housemaids' chorus in *Don Pasquale*: blue packages were lifted, hoisted onto shoulders, onto heads: and in no time the bearers vanished, leaving the cloister floor empty. Another brief order: the coffee-maker opened her till and beckoned to the porter; pocketing and saluting, he left the stage. "And now," the Superior said to Ladislao, "please give my thanks to these gentlemen, and I hope that they and you will partake of our poor hospitality."

Ladislao looked at the coffee-nun, already busy at her levers. A vague memory reached him: the same face, beside a similar machine elsewhere . . . He was interrupted by a harsh voice.

"*Hey. You.*"

He turned. All four were looking at him.

"What'd she say?"

"She's offering us coffee."

"She's offering us *what?*"

"Coffee."

"And what about the rest?"

"All in good time. She . . ."

"Who's got good time? Get hold of it."

Ladislao hesitated. In Naples, absence of hurry and pressure was apt to result in a better price, but the quartet gave no evidence of being in a mood to be told so.

"Get hold of it. We're due back."

There seemed to be nothing for it.

"Reverend Mother, these gentlemen must return to their duties. They would appreciate . . ."

"Something other than coffee? A liqueur? I am grateful for their gift."

Gift!

"What would they like? What can I offer them?"

"Just the going rate, Madre." The manager had got the Nessiemen to agree to that. "It's quite understood they'll accept whatever you've been in the habit of paying."

"*Paying!*"

"What you are accustomed to pay for the product."

"*Pay!* For an unsolicited gift! Young man . . ."

Ladislao liked less and less the looks on the faces of the four. "Reverend Mother . . ."

The next few minutes were a kaleidoscope. The nun's

reiteration that she had received no notice of an impending visit, had expected no one; Ladislao's realization that Vispo had not telephoned as promised to announce their coming; that Vispo's "change of plan" consisted of transforming the scheduled swindle-and-drubbing of the Nessiemen at Swank into this swindle of them at the convent, certain to be followed by their retaliatory drubbing of Ladislao himself; his swearing to the four that he was innocent; their snarling and snapping and asking whether he thought they were born yesterday. From the squalid sequence, Ladislao withdrew into himself, and manifested the seigneurial manner of which he had a strong, if little displayed, reserve. "What do you want to do?" he asked in cold sarcasm. "Search the convent?"

Search the convent!

How was Ladislao, citizen of a land where nuns were people everyone knew—relatives, friends, acquaintances like anyone else, dressed differently—to foresee the outrage of these Irish-Americans whose sisters, cousins and aunts in convents from Boston to San Francisco had been transformed by their vows into holy beings, sanctified and set apart; utterly different, though today they might have stopped dressing differently, from the rest of the world? Even the ironic suggestion that a convent might be searched was sacrilege to these Knights of Columbus.

"A heathen!"

"A perv, I guess!"

Sister Silena was looking on with an anxiety not shown by the Reverend Mother, who was simply watching. The coffee-nun said a few words. After a moment Reverend Mother spoke. "You are in difficulty with your associates?"

"Is there a back way out?"

"Tell them I'll go with you."

"Reverend Mother is going to telephone," he said. "To the Consortium. I'll talk to them too, and get them to explain things to her. We'll work something out. Keep your shirts on." (NATO radio again.)

He had feared that one or two might insist on accompanying them, but this time their awe of the vestals' sancta sanctorum worked in his favor. Reverend Mother led him down a series of corridors, and at the small door she opened for him she asked where he was going.

"Villa Bklyn."

"Villa Bklyn! You know those Saccas?"

"A friend of mine lives at Villa Bklyn. Which way, please?"

She told him about the turnings.

"How will you handle the men, Madre? They're dangerous."

"Not to me. Who are they?"

"From the yacht."

"What yacht? No matter. You'd better go."

As she shut the door behind him he heard her say, "God keep you."

He set off down the whitewashed alley. Turn right. Turn left. What a maze!

He hoped that by the time he arrived at Villa Bklyn the other guest wouldn't have left—the one whose visit to the Professor he himself had arranged for, necessarily without the Professor's knowledge. Out of the conversation the three of them would have, although its prime subject was to have been something different, perhaps a suggestion would emerge to help him escape from the double threat suddenly looming.

What would have happened, once outside the convent, had he left with the Nessiemen? How vicious would the pummeling in a nearby alley have been? Vispo couldn't have foreseen that they would leave their guns behind. Had he perhaps envisaged their using them? Vispo himself would have been quite in the clear.

What would happen now? Would Vispo feign astonishment when they next met, express regrets for a "misunderstanding," blame the manager for having "forgotten" to telephone the Reverend Mother? Once or twice, when the jukebox in the palazzo had been playing lower than usual, Ladislao had heard Vispo speak on the telephone, or to an unfortunate "guest" in the Club room, about "misunderstandings," in a tone he had come to recognize.

Certainly he and Melba had been stupid, beyond the point of innocence: they had had their own wits to go by, and there had been those remarks by the palazzo's old tenants. Today's trick . . . Had it been intended, in case of survival, as a warning? A warning of what? To one? To both? In case of non-survival, what was its message to Melba?

THE WHITE ALLEYS were a labyrinth. Trying to keep to a direction, he was confused by medieval curves and corners, blocked by a series of culs-de-sac; plunging into a courtyard, he scattered a family of cats eating from fishy paper. Where was he? How to find the street, the street the nun said would lead straight to Villa Bklyn? This turning, perhaps? It gave promise of widening, of opening out into a thoroughfare.

It did indeed: he was back in the square before the church: and not twenty yards away four men in black were just emerging from the convent door. There was shouting, a surge in his direction. Twisting, he ran back into the web of alleys.

The loudspeakers on the church were reverberating:

> *But it was Mary, Mary, long before the fashions came;*
> *And there's something there*
> *That sounds so fair,*
> *It's a grand old name!*

31

THE RING at the gate took Nat to the top of the stairs.

It was the red-haired cooper or Cooper last seen standing on the altar in the *Nessie's* chapel. "I'm relieved to find myself in the right place, Professor. The young man gave me directions, but I was beginning to fear my thoughts hadn't kept the roadway." Instead of the Cockney he had used for cursing the obstinate altarpiece, he was speaking ordinary middle-class British English. On the terrace, while Nat murmured his one-sided introduction to Melba, the unexpected guest looked about. "The English-speaking Italian lad isn't here? I say, I'm afraid I'm interrupting . . ."

Wondering what had brought him, Nat made an effort to emerge from the abstraction induced by Melba's words. Reflections inspired by her remark about working one's way through college. She had been candid about what kind of an organization the "Club" was: yet what she had expressed was not regret or concern, but defensiveness, that the nephew she had raised from infancy should be associated with it. She was right, of course, about American students not always being nicely employed. Nat himself, when adviser at the university, had been entrusted with some surprising confidences. But despite Melba's cry at Swank—"Is Laddie all right, at least?"—there seemed to be less intense alarm than might be expected over the boy's very presence in a situation where his *not* being "all right" was an easy possibility.

The visitor from the *Nessie*, when Nat could finally give him full attention, proved to be both Cooper and cooper—"Being nautical for 'handyman,' no name fits my nature but my own." His words about Ladislao now brought a question from Melba to Nat. On hearing the answer—that yes, Ladislao had said he'd be coming, but not when—the cooper drew an envelope from a pocket and a photograph from the envelope. "I don't think I have to wait until he arrives to show you this, Professor. You're the one he said would be interested. I had this photograph propped up on the altar and he spotted it. He said that in the confusion you didn't notice."

Politely he handed the photo to Melba. She cried "Dio!" and passed it to Nat.

He too was startled. "How come you have this, Mr. Cooper?"

"Madam's latest purchase, Professor. Latest in the art field, that is. I don't count the daily harvest of branched velvet gowns."

Melba extracted a folded clipping from her purse and opened it on the table. Beside the cooper's fresh glossy print, the newspaper illustration was dim: but both showed the same Madonna. On the reverse of the glossy were written the names of the Midwestern Educational Institution and of Mrs. Kaloumian, and of art dealers in Chicago and Rome. At the bottom, a notation in inches and centimeters.

The picture, of unknown late Renaissance authorship, was one of the more popular of old Deming's finds. Quite often reproduced, its de-accessioning even by the recidivistic Institution seemed astonishing. Concentrated reflection suggested a reason, perhaps farfetched. Unlike the majority of the collection, this was no primitive, but a Mannerist work, anything but "non-relevant to current taste." This might posit, as its discarder, an aggressively forward-looking member of the Gallery staff, who suspected that this picture's era of high favor might be approaching its end and was determined to keep ahead of the game. Experts of that kind, to whom the title "curator" is dubiously applicable, are on the increase.

"You catch the resemblance to Mrs. K., Professor? I imagine that must play a part."

The Madonna's head was indeed noticeably Brennan-like,

her hair a tawny mass, her expression strangely brooding. For an irreverent moment Nat saw Lyle in drag.

"It's coming to the island?"

"To the *Nessie* this very night, Professor. You see they've supplied dimensions for my guidance. I'm to hang it where you taught the remover to remove."

Just as Nat recognized the last words as the key to what he had already registered as a singular habit of speech, the street bell rang again.

LYLE WAS on the steps, in full spate, calling even as he climbed: "Nat! You knew I'd come. I didn't even stop at the hotel to change. Give me a blow-by-blow about the *Nessie*, please. Tell me all."

He quieted at the sight of the others. The cooper looked with curiosity at the newcomer who spoke of his ship; introductions were performed. Nat hadn't thought to be giving such a party.

Seeing Lyle's eye light on the photographs, he identified them as having been brought to display "Mrs. Kaloumian's new altarpiece for the ship's chapel," leaving Lyle to mention his connection if he wished. He did not do so: taking up both pictures he merely remarked, after a glance at the newspaper article, "Julia's university. She's a trustee."

Here was a more probable reason for the de-accessioning. The Institution might even have preferred to retain the picture, but considered it politic not to oppose, in the atmosphere generated by its own policy of discard, the covetousness of a trustee, especially as powerful a one as Mrs. Kaloumian. Who would have been advised, of course, by someone in the know—doubtless the Chicago dealer mentioned on the back of the glossy—of the picture's desirability.

Lyle's tone became less casual as he studied the photographs. He asked Nat's earlier question: "You mean this is coming here?"

The cooper seemed happy to answer again. "Tonight. Mrs. K. and guests arrive with the picture by seaplane after dining in

Rome. I'll be in the chapel till the bird of dawning singeth: Our Lady has to be in place for tomorrow. Madam's birthday. You heard the broadcast from the church?"

Once again Melba cried "Dio!" And: "The 'Happy Birthday'! It's for her?"

"Didn't you catch the 'Julia'? A day early, actually. Somebody goofed by twenty-four hours."

" A broadcast about Julia? A celebration?" Now Lyle sounded anything but casual. "That's right. I'd forgotten about her birthday."

"Hark where it comes again!"

The cooper's mention had reinvoked the polyphony. The air throbbed with bells, with organ, and finally:

> *Hap-py Birth-day, dear Jooool-ya*
> *Hap-py Birth-day toooo yooooo!*

Lyle had discarded the newspaper, but continued to stare at the glossy. His "How absolutely marvelous!" as the last of the clangor died away might have been taken to refer to the serenade, had he not added: "It does reproduce splendidly, doesn't it. Where will the seaplane land?"

"Outside the breakwater. The dinghy will be ready to ferry the party aboard, together with my long night's work. Such is the program." The cooper stood up. "Return I must. I hear the howling of Irish-American wolves."

Nat went with him to the top of the stairs. "I wonder whether I've guessed the reason for the change of altarpiece. Is it because the subject of the old one was found to be . . ."

". . . pagan? You spotted it. An art bloke from her museum broke the news to her when he was a guest on the yacht a couple of months ago. A daub, he said. 'Not worthy of you, Mrs. K., and nothing to do with Saint Laurence.' Neptune and his trident. You should have heard her language on the telephone when she got the dealer who sold it to her. I was tending switchboard. He was a match for her. 'Of course it's just a dirty smear, Mrs. K. Smear for smear, Mrs. K.' Before she hung up on him I heard him tell her he was the brother of somebody she and her first husband screwed at a houseparty somewhere. Runs his art business under a company name. He rubbed it in and loved it."

Lyle had joined them in time to hear the last. "That was one of the famous Washington stories. The Goodspeeds got their weekend hostess to invite a senator they didn't like, without his wife, and set up a badger game right there in the house. Then leaked it to the press. The poor fool lost his seat *and* his wife. I've always credited Julia with the masterminding."

"You sound as though you know the lady quite well, Sir. *Brennan!* You wouldn't be the man of the book?"

"Afraid so."

"Oho! You haven't gone unmentioned on board, Sir. I'll tell you that. Well, I'm off."

Lyle, it seemed, was leaving too, and he and the cooper went down the stairs together.

32

"WHAT A horrid man!"

"Which one do you mean?"

"That should be obvious, I think. I was glad to see him go. The one who was fascinated by our picture."

He might have misheard, but he hadn't.

"I'll never think of it as anybody's but the family's, you know."

"I feel rather possessive about it myself. It's the frontispiece of my book."

"I know. Think of its coming so close! One of them coming right to us!"

He remembered her saying, "Now that they're being dispersed what hope remains?" Had Melba really had that hope?

"By 'close' you mean back to the land of its birth." Fending her off.

"Not at all. I mean close to me. To you, too, in a way, since you're you and happen to be here: that makes it all the stranger. To Palazzo Rovigliano, really, where it belongs. Your friend stared at it as though he'd like to gobble it up himself."

"You can be sure his only interest in it is through Mrs. Kaloumian. She's his cousin. They had a falling-out some time ago, and he's trying for a reconciliation, or at least a confrontation. Sniffing around. You heard him ask about the yacht. Now it's her new picture."

"*Her* new picture!"

"The dispersal is shameful, as we said before."

"They have no right."

"No more moral right to disperse as they're doing than to acquire as they did. But what's to be done if curators and trustees agree once again after a hundred years?"

"Then it's up to us!"

"Us?"

"People like us. People who know what's right. You and your book defending my grandfather. My brother. If my brother were here now, with one of them coming so close . . ."

"What would he do?"

"His best. As he did. He failed. But now there's Laddie. Laddie will do anything for me. Anything I ask. And you—you're for me, I know. You'll help me."

Melba was transformed, exalted.

It probably would have been better to let her assume that he understood what she was driving at, what it was she had in mind. And keep her talking or otherwise distracted until Ladislao himself arrived and could take charge of her. Having lived with her all his twenty years the boy would know what to do. It was unlikely that this was her first show of delusion. But instead he heard himself say sharply: "Ladislao must under no circumstances have anything to do with it." Without having any clear idea of what "it" might be: only a flash of a boy fighting off a pack of howling wolves.

She flushed. "Laddie knows what the family feeling has always been. I thought you did, too."

"You know I do. But . . ."

" 'But!' I understand. I confess that from you I'd hoped for more than 'but.' Fortunately there are others to turn to."

So that was what she meant! Was she serious?

Her anger took him back over the years to another "But . . ." consequent on old Deming. The trimming university president, that day, hearing the rejection of his "But Professor Haley . . . ," had probably comforted himself by deciding that his assistant professor was fanatical. But there are real fanatics—dangerous, some of them—who know how to make anyone feel like a trimmer.

They made uneasy talk for a while, both of them longing for Ladislao's arrival, Melba's demeanor openly scornful. When she said she could wait no longer Nat set out with her, escorting her in almost total silence back to the hotel. They exchanged stiff farewells. She said that she and Ladislao would be returning to Naples in the morning.

NOT ONLY during the last minutes with Melba, but all afternoon, Nat had been impatient for Ladislao's ring. He had expected it would herald closer acquaintance with this suddenly discovered unknown who had heard about him all his life—actually, it seemed, been to some extent "brought up on" him. The boy had not come, and now would be leaving the island. Palazzo Rovigliano was only half an hour away on the mainland, but such very fragmentary first meetings as theirs could scarcely prosper once interrupted and transplanted: ripening came not from repetition, but with continuity. As he thought of this great-grandson of old Deming—and thinking too of childlessness, as he so often did these days—there came to him a phrase of Lyle Brennan's: what was young Rovigliano if not a "living sequel"?

33

Lyle was by experience quick to detect, usually through mannerisms of speech, the mark of a possible media "personality." Unlike Nat, he had not identified the source of some of the cooper's parlance, but he had easily spotted the man's true profession, and as they walked back toward the village from Villa Bklyn he asked whether he had ever been tested for the home screen.

"Playing the Comedies, Histories and Tragedies up and down the English provinces doesn't automatically bring the BBC to the door, Mr. Brennan. On starvation wages one's bones grow marrowless, and one's lucky to be at the head of the queue in a little port when the *Nessie* suddenly calls for a handyman because—as one learns later—one's predecessor was sent to hospital after letting slip to his colleagues a few thoughtless words about Hibernian politics."

" '*Celebrated Actor Hired as Kaloumians' Handyman.*' Like it? I've been asked to do a series of what we're calling Guest Profiles, and next week I'm flying to New York to tape a few. Would you consider coming along for a try?"

"Would I not."

Lyle mentioned a fee, swollen for his purpose. "It's by no means a fortune—"

"Comparative term."

"—and I can't promise anything beyond. Do you think you could get leave from the *Nessie?*"

"Consider it got."

So much for that. No great accomplishment. Actors stuck in the humdrum come unstuck easy.

Now for the other, more crucial, conversational drift, as casual-seeming as possible.

In preparation, Lyle silently went over the ground, his mind rehearsing in media jargon. The arrival of a planeful of guests meant that Julia would be constantly surrounded. His chances of waylaying her for a *meaningful dialogue* that he could surreptitiously tape or otherwise report over the airwaves were slimmer than he had hoped. Her acquisition of the extraordinarily photogenic Madonna suggested a *different scenario.* One that would necessitate neither reconciliation nor hostility but could be made to hint at either. It would have the advantage of creating a *permanent visual record*, splendidly reproducible in the media. Its actuality firmly anchored in photographs taken on board the *Nessie* itself, and in the skillful exploitation of a picturesque cooper, it would be an *unusually unique video feature.*

"Did I understand you to say you'd be working all night installing the picture?"

"Essential to become a borrower of the night. Since the Queen of Heaven must be in place ere glow-worm shows the matin to be near."

Lyle didn't get even that pair, overdone for his benefit though they were. "Rather eerie, I should think, working alone on an otherwise sleeping ship."

"On the *Nessie*, no company's the best."

"*Psst!*"

Ridiculous sound. Ridiculous sight. Last Sunday's blond

teaser, ungrateful little brute, peering and beckoning from just inside an alley. Burlesque of a moment in melodrama. Almost Verdian. Extract from The Story of the Opera: "The angelo who turned out to be in the pay of the police and then proclaimed himself the son of a duke hisses from his hiding place." The boy who was apparently in some way a find for poor old psychographer Nat Haley, himself shamelessly mooning around Italy with his widower's heart on his sleeve. And in what a state the child was. Disheveled, sweaty, doubtless gamy.

"*Psst!*"

Lyle would have walked on, paying him as little notice as he deserved. But the cooper stopped. "Heigh-ho! What kept you? I thought we were meeting at the Prof's."

"You're coming from Villa Bklyn? Have the men been there?"

"The men?"

"From the *Nessie*. Any sign of them?"

"You confuse me. I thought you were the one who'd be seeing them this afternoon, before meeting me."

The boy was breathless. "Is everything clear between here and the villa? They've been crossing and recrossing this street for the last half hour. Patrolling. I couldn't get through."

"Pardon, Master. For my more sweet understanding. My shipmates turned on you? Why?"

The soi-disant dukeling said something complex and tedious about a "double doublecross." "They have every reason to be bloody-minded about me, and I've got to keep out of their way."

"In that case you'll either have to hole up or leave this war-like isle," the cooper told him. "Because we'll certainly be here for the next few days. But just now I think the Sinn Feiners must be down at the port. The dinghy's picking us up there almost immediately. Last shore call of the day."

Lyle wished he were less susceptible. Even in disarray the

young fellow was tantalizing. "We've just come," he said, quite against his resolution, "from seeing your aunt."

That seemed positively to stagger the boy, but he continued to address the cooper. "My aunt was at the villa? I'd never have had you show the photograph anyplace where she was. Did it upset her?"

Lyle persisted. "Excited her, I'd say. To the point of hating me because I looked at it too."

"I must get to her," the boy told the cooper.

"I wonder whether something I've thought of might interest you and your aunt, Duca. I'm flying home next week to do a television documentary on the Kaloumians. Mr. Cooper has kindly consented to participate. Titles are much appreciated in the States. 'Ducal Family Former Owners of Mrs. K.'s New Madonna.' Just a few words from each of you about the background and your present feelings about the picture. You'd both be so charming. We'd fly you, of course. A week in New York . . ."

There was no sign that he had heard. "You left her at Professor Haley's?" He was now standing as for flight.

"We did. Yes." And the cooper continued: "Look: we're almost at the piazza. Run out to the belvedere and check that they're down at the port. Then you'll know you have a freeway to the villa."

The boy was gone in an instant.

"I KNOW YOU'RE due at the dock," Lyle said. "So why don't I take the funicular down with you? We can talk on the way."

As they descended, he found he had to confide in the cooper a little more than he would have preferred.

"All I want," he said finally, "is a few good negatives of you and me—especially me—on board, with the picture. Don't you think the hour I suggest would be the best?"

"To get to shipboard undescried? While they're all snoring on down pillows?" The cooper pondered. "I do get along pretty well with the night man. We could try. On the other hand, I think I may have a better idea."

34

LADISLAO PRESSED the bell with the Professor's name beside it and ran up the stairs. On a terrace off the first landing a nice-looking old couple was sitting in the shade among masses of geraniums. A pleasant sight. The lady was knitting; the gentleman greeted him by wagging an upward-pointed finger and saying "Out."

"Oh—I was told they were . . ."

"Five minutes ago."

He knew he must look the way he felt, when the lady rose quickly and said she'd fetch a glass. "You're overheated, Signorino. Sit down. Rest yourself."

He sank onto a chair and wiped his streaming face. On a table was a cool-looking carafe, and when the glass came he gulped what the old lady poured for him. She went out again and returned with a basin and a towel. It was something a mother in the palazzo courtyard might have done for her hurt child.

"Suddenly the Professore has friends," said the gentleman. "You're the fourth today."

Here on their terrace halfway up to the Professor's they had an air of presiding like faithful porters, a pair of friendly watch-dogs.

His thirst relieved, his skin cooler, he remembered his manners. "Rovigliano."

"Sacca. My sister." The ritual handshakes. "Are you related to the lady who was with the Professore?"

"My aunt. I expected to find her here."

"You must have missed them on the road. They probably took one of the little streets. The Professore knows the island very well. He's learned a few things about it from us, hasn't he, Immacolatina? Things the tourists don't hear about."

The air throbbed. The same clamorous bells as earlier in the day. Then the organ. And the tremendous voice:

Hap-py Birth-day toooo yoooo!

"———! ——— ———! ———! ———!"

"Roberto! Calm! Calm yourself!"

The old gentleman was coughing, choking on his own fury.

After a recuperative pause: "That abomination, for example. The Professore was surprised, wasn't he, Immacolatina, when we told him about Fedora and the Parroco."

"My brother is speaking of the Mother Superior of our convent, Madre Serafina."

"Madre Serafina!" He remembered. "When I told her I was coming here she asked if I knew you."

"You saw Serafina?"

"Today—on business."

"She asked because she's our cousin." The old lady laughed. "Aunts, cousins. See how quickly we learn about each other! No secrets on this little island!"

Signor Sacca said: "On business?"

It was time to go. Tell no more. He shouldn't have said that much—on this little island. *"Yes, he saw her on business, and his aunt saw her on business, and the Professore saw his aunt, and . . ."* "Now I must hurry on. To find my aunt. Forgive my leaving so abruptly. Thank you . . ."

"On business, you said?"

"Good-bye. Thank you both a thousand times. Good-bye, Signora."

"Signorina."

"Good-bye, Signorina. Good-bye, Signore."

"Good-bye, good-bye."

HE REMEMBERED the Professor saying on the *Nessie*, "Ask at the Imperatore," and his mute answer that to go there was for him unthinkable. Now he must get there quickly. Already he regretted his few minutes' rest and cursed the delays that had preceded it. Had he arrived earlier at Villa Bklyn he might have prevented the encounter between Melba and the picture—the unforeseen, dangerous transformation of what he had arranged as an exhibition for the Professor alone. At least he could have tried to deal with Melba's "excitement," as the invertito called it. Hitherto, Melba's periodic fits about the pictures had been staged in a total absence of pictures, and he had become adept at cajoling her back to tranquillity. But now that there actually was a picture . . . He told himself to expect anything.

Approaching the hotel, he glanced up at the crowded tables on the streetside terrace. There they were: Melba and Vispo together. As he mounted the few steps he saw Mario, the capo, in his jacket and gold braid; and he saw Mario recognize him, frown, and start forward. Today, he supposed, Mario must regard him as even more of a pariah than at that cocktail time last week, a few hours before the first explosion, when he was called out from the pantry in his dirty apron to take a telephone call. Now, on seeing him join the two guests, one of whom kissed him, Mario came no further; but he kept watching. Vispo was saying to Melba: ". . . organize an operation like that out of a pure blue sky?"

". . . da ciel sereno?" As Vispo uttered those last words

Ladislao saw Mario turn to Carlo, the waiter, and Carlo was at the table in an instant."

"Ciao, Carlo."

"Commandi, Signore." No recognition, nothing but deference, as he took Ladislao's order. A few nights before, he'd been telling him dirty stories about the guests.

"Well, Don Ladì, how did things go at the convent?" Like Melba, Vispo had bought new clothes for the visit to the island, and leaning back in his chair he looked as easy as anyone else in the cocktail crowd—the men in summer sports clothes, women sleek and lovely in long bright dresses. And Vispo's very smile had something new about it.

"Less well than you'd hoped, brother. As you see, I'm still alive and unbruised." That would have been one way to answer. But he said: "Like a charm. Reverend Mother blessed the Nessiemen for their generosity and let them kiss her ring. Both parties were thrilled. The whole thing was a brilliant idea of yours."

A briefly uncertain glance; then appreciation of the answer was conveyed by a chilling laugh. Meanwhile, Melba was asking: "The convent, caro? Here on the island? You've been at the convent?"

"He did a little errand for me there, Principessa. Shortly after you did yours."

"You saw Fedo . . . the Reverend Mother?"

"Madre Serafina, yes. My errand was with her."

"Did you tell her your . . . ? Did you mention me?"

"That was how I introduced myself. As your nephew. Since I knew you'd just been there. Why? Shouldn't I have?"

He looked from one to the other, the hollow sensation briefly returning. Vispo, who had hunted out the birth certificate, had it copied, and left it outside his door, was looking at them both. Ladislao repeated: "Is there some reason I shouldn't have told her about being your nephew?"

"Heavens no, caro, no. I just wondered. It must have seemed

a strange coincidence to her, that's all, don't you think, that we should both visit her the same day?"

"Aunt Melba has been telling me about the picture suddenly turning up, Ladì," Vispo said. "I agree with her that it should return to the family, at least temporarily. As a member of the family myself, I feel strongly about it, and I imagine you do too."

Ladislao had to force himself to believe it was Vispo speaking. The new Vispo: the change was too abrupt, too obviously concurrent with other details, not to be part of the threat. And Melba was accepting the new form of address as though ready for it. He saw the turn the "excitement" was taking.

"This does indeed seem an excellent opportunity." Vispo's pompous tone was suited to an important family conference. "But as I've been telling Aunt Melba, the kind of operation it requires should have had advance planning. Especially since it's outside our usual range. There's so little time. I don't know . . . I'm thinking of one possibility. There's the Consortium's other arm—its right arm, so to speak: we of the Salt Committee are only the left, compared with them. They might be willing to do it for us, as a novelty. Being water-borne, they're better equipped. As I see it, it might go something like this. . . ."

The expressions on Melba's face, as he watched her during Vispo's outline that followed, brought back her joyful reading of his school reports; or the way, after completing her early assignments for the Club, she used to come home waving her bankbook, and he'd know she had deposited something more to keep them going—and him at his studies.

Vispo finished. "We could try that."

Radiant was the word for Melba.

"*Prison.*" Ladislao stressed the word without raising his voice. "Prison, Melba. We'd all go there, you know. *Prison. P-r-i-g-i-o-n-e.*"

But even before he began to spell, the loudspeakers on the church were splintering the island air with vesper-song. Mixed voices brayed:

As they sat silent, waiting it out, Ladislao knew that Melba had heard little of what he said. He recalled a recent item of Neapolitan news: an up-to-date women's prison had been installed in what had been the old insane asylum.

Vispo had heard. And in his repetition of his strange new smile Ladislao read the answer: *"All* of us wouldn't go." What Vispo actually said was: "I wouldn't worry about that, Aunt Melba. We'd almost certainly find somebody to take the picture off your hands. The idea wouldn't be to keep it—just to get it back, then unload it appropriately. Are you afraid of jail, Ladì? You went like a lamb the other day—a step in helping with your education, wasn't it? An education must be a precious thing, I've always thought. Wouldn't you risk it again? We could probably get you out as quickly as the last time—if we really tried."

Melba was hearing only what she wanted to hear. He could see only one way: to play along, miming reluctant consent, and invent some means of bringing her to her senses before it was too late.

"Oh, I wouldn't keep it for a single day!" she was saying. "I'd give it away! To a church! To a convent! Just so it's ours again first, as it should be!"

"Give it away? That scarcely makes sense, Aunt Melba. There is a market for such things. You're too idealistic, if I may say so. If there's no practical advantage, I say let's forget it."

He knew how to spur her on.

"No, no. We must. It's come too close not to. It's been sent to us. Heaven-sent. Sent by . . ."

"Let's say fate, Aunt Melba. Ladì will go with the spidermen, to point out just what it is that interests us."

"Oh, he will! You will, caro, you will, won't you, of course!"

The same Melba whom he had heard say over the telephone in this same bar, "I feel need of reassurance."

"Because the spidermen might easily fail to recognize an object of that kind," Vispo said. "It's not like anything they deal in. Especially when it's wrapped up, as I suppose it will be."

In her agitation Melba swept her glass from the table. Mario, still hovering, snapped his fingers, and Carlo came quickly with broom and dustpan.

"I'll telephone the spidermen now. By the way, Ladì, a question. Where will you sleep tonight? I'll try to persuade the spidermen to run you out to Swank after the operation's over, but that's a little out of their way, and it will be late: they'll be wanting to get on to Naples. You could go to Naples with them if you liked. Your work here is finished. Everybody will be going home tomorrow anyway."

He had been wondering about his next bed. From the jail, he'd been taken to Swank, and had been sleeping there on a cot beside those set up for the Club members. Among "friends," he had supposed. But if the Nessiemen missed him the next time, who knew what role those bedfellows might be assigned? On the other hand, the dark crossing to Naples in the speedboat with the spidermen . . . A third band of saints to do Vispo's work! Would a few words suggesting that solution perhaps be included in the telephone call his half brother was now about to make?

"We could let my sleeping place depend on where we deliver the merchandise."

"Excellent! Spoken like a Club director! Maybe you and I should exchange places, Ladì. You've no idea how I always wanted to go to the university."

It was among the textbooks that he had slipped the birth certificate.

He left them alone.

"Isn't it marvelous, caro, that this should be happening at last? I'm so happy."

One more attempt. "Melba, listen. *Listen.*"

Suddenly Mario was murmuring beside him. "Professor

Haley telephoned. He thought you might come here. In case I saw you, if I could get your ear alone: he has just learned you were at the villa, and suggests that you return, have dinner with him. If he's not there, wait." All said amid the rearranging of glasses, the removal of a dish, the flicking of a napkin.

"What did he say, caro? Did I hear him mention Professor Haley? I have to tell you I'm disappointed in Professor Haley. I thought he would be the first to understand. But he . . . ."

"Melba, *listen.*"

Hopeless. To press too hard would only delay the swing back to normal—if there was to be a return this time. The Professor, he gathered, must have spoken much as he himself was speaking now, and had got about as far. His own meeting with the Professor would have to be postponed, for here was his half brother back. "Come along, Ladì. The spidermen accept. We'll go and brief them. They're sending a boat. We have a little walk first."

"Good-bye, caro. Have you a sweater?" He waved his red pullover at her. It was as though he were going off to play tennis. He thought of something that always amused him: the most snobbish Naples tennis club, the one he was sometimes invited to by friends, was called Il Tennyson. "Oh," he heard her call, "how proud of you Duca would be!"

35

Sacca was just coming down the stairs of Villa Bklyn as Nat returned after leaving Melba. *"Salve!"* He gave Nat a closer look. "You're tired, Professore! Guests! Hospitality without a hostess! My sister and I were speaking of it. It's not right. Not right! Let me invite you, Professore. Come with me now on a little boat ride I'm about to take. Just an hour. It will be refreshing. Give you a change. Dusk is pleasant on the water."

A man-to-man invitation, scarcely consistent with the words preceding it. But a welcome opportunity to shed the day's sordid events, an excuse not to return in low spirits to an empty flat. Turning round, he accompanied his landlord to the funicular. They had reached the marina and were about to step into a water taxi when Sacca tapped a finger to his forehead. "About your guests, Professore. I forgot to tell you: there was another one. A signorino. He . . ."

"A signorino?"

"Who looks like his aunt. And who came . . ."

"He came!"

". . . looking for her, though it was you he first asked for. And went off almost at once to find her."

"No message?"

"Only that he must find his aunt."

"Excuse me. Excuse me while I telephone."

The message Nat left with Mario from the booth on the waterfront was the best device he could think of for seeing the boy again—the descendant of old Deming who by coming to the villa had shown himself not totally indifferent to the fact of their paths having crossed. Now there was particular reason to meet: drama was in the making, and the young protagonist might benefit from a few words of warning. Nat could scarcely rush to the Imperatore, break into the three-cornered talk Mario told him was under way at a table on the terrace, and constitute himself the boy's protector: he didn't absolutely know that Ladislao needed, or wanted, protection. But he could at least leave word that he was welcome at Villa Bklyn.

"Sheep ahoy!" Sacca cried, as they cast off. He laughed, saying he knew he was using the phrase incorrectly, but at least not insultingly, like the former tenants of Nat's apartment from whom he had learned it—another American, "slightly alcoholic," as was also his wife. Together that pair had shouted the words from their terrace whenever they spied a large local lady, balancing a burden on her head in the usual island way, passing in the street below. That couple had been asked to leave Villa Bklyn. "They were your opposites, Professore. On this vacation island a landlord seldom gets a tenant as well behaved as you, so quiet that sometimes my sister and I wonder if you've died up there and gone to heaven."

Nat was beginning to be irked by Sacca's remarks on his staid behavior. This one, extreme in suggesting extinction, reminded him—perhaps because they were coming within view of a cove he recognized as the Cala—of Lyle's remarks about the "deadliness" of scholarly pursuits.

This evening the Cala was in shadow, the sun having sunk below its background hemi-cycle of cliffs. A single craft was to be seen, moored at the jetty: a black one, black even against the blackness of the water. Nat recognized it for what it was. "Is the Cala the rendezvous of the spiders, then? I've always wondered where they set out from."

The islander at the helm looked up and laughed, and Sacca said merely, "Pazienza."

It was difficult to think of this dark, even sinister Cala as the blazing sun-trap it had been the other morning. Now dankness seemed to issue from it, chilling them as they floated past. Nat had never before seen it from without; down the side of one steep slope the zigzag path of access was a scar amid the scrub. Two figures, perhaps late bathers, one of them a speck of red, were visible toward the top: he hoped that they were climbing up into the light—he himself would not have liked to be descending there at this hour.

Beyond the farther of the Cala's embracing cliffs the coast continued craggy and rugged, the limestone perforated by a series of grottoes, some at sea level, some above. Passing a jagged promontory, they turned sharply inward, heading toward what seemed a total blackness of water and rock. So deep was the shadow that they were in the cave before Nat knew it was there.

Someone ahead of them laughed and said, "Rent day again!"; and he saw that they were inching forward in smooth water that continued deep inside the arched opening of the grotto and ended at a natural barrier, a shelf of rock standing several feet above sea level. The lock-like water chamber easily accommodated the several black spiders moored side by side, like so many heavier, less graceful gondolas, their sterns protected by rubber-tire buffers suspended from the wall. Gradually he discerned, in the far background, stalagmites and stalactites; overhead, a ceiling of uneven natural stone studded here and there with tufts of lichen; and on the shelf, amid a decor of rough tables and chairs, cookstove, electric wires, gasoline pump and telephone, a costume party of about a dozen men. In their bestiality their faces resembled those of the Nessiemen and the members of Melba's "Club"; but these men had got themselves up theatrically. Grotesquely cut beards and moustaches; strange hats and caps; bright sashes, earrings, chains of true or false silver and gold; and a few had wrapped their heads in bandannas à la Carmen. Few deigned to show that they had noticed the boat's arrival: dressed for their parts, they displayed the aggressive indifference of actors toward those outside the profession.

Sacca's usual ebullience was stilled. He sat quietly in the boat and waited. The helmsman had not tied up, but held his rope looped around a rung of the ladder mounting to the shelf. After a time there advanced from the rear one not in costume who leaned down and exchanged with Sacca a handshake that was no mere meeting of empty palms. Nat understood some of their brief dialogue: the wiring of the rented grotto was faulty, and Sacca as landlord promised to have it repaired. A few bare parting words, and they took their last glimpse of the gypsy or pirate pantomime.

No word was spoken in the little boat until they were well away; then Sacca broached a variation of his earlier theme.

"You were an admirably silent spectator, Professore. You're the only person I've ever invited on one of these little business trips: I knew you'd behave perfectly. One observes prudence with those people. What did you think of that close-up of our island specialty?"

The answer to the question which Nat, in turn, was about to ask—why grottoes should be bothered with at all, if as hideaways they were all as open as that one—was provided by Sacca's comment on a spectacle which just then began to unfold a few hundred yards away. The wail of a siren came from behind them and was answered by another, ahead; from the direction of the Cala there dashed into view a single black spider, its wash brilliant in the dusk. And then, from opposite directions, sirens continuing to wail, appeared twin gray coast guard launches, which simultaneously switched on their searchlights, catching the spider in the crossbeam. A sound of shots, and the launches closed in on their prey.

In the little boat the helmsman was laughing. Sacca began to recite what he prophesied would be "a very brief item" in the Naples press the next day: " '. . . *Halted only after gunfire, the craft under suspicion was nevertheless found to be carrying no cargo. Its papers and those of its crew being in perfect order, it was allowed to go on its way.* They flash some kind of signal when they're empty, Professore, and those are the ones the coast guard stops. The firing is into the air, of course. Duty faithfully done. The paper will print the names of the intrepid coast guard officers. And all of us who read know what the true story is. Opera buffa! Buffissima!"

Until lost from view, they saw the trio of boats, the two hunters and the captive, remain close together on the water, as though in conversation.

"In the performance of their business, however, there's no make-believe, Professore. Those men know how to load their boats and get their cargoes to Naples. Don't let the fancy dress fool you." The tone veered close to admiration.

"We have dress-up gangs at home. A special kink. Ours can be deadly."

"These would be, too, on their own. The Consortium performs a public service in keeping them busy under its orders. It recognizes that such men have to earn their living, like the rest of us."

Nat listened and looked in the expectation—at least the hope—of finding irony in that apology for drug traffic. He found none. Sacca added: "It's all part of keeping the island such a peaceful place."

Dark had fallen when they returned to the marina. Out beyond the breakwater were the lights of the *Nessie.*

36

LYLE BRENNAN shivered. He was chilled through the thin raincoat, the short-sleeved shirt, the white duck slacks. Only his head was well protected, under the stiff-visored officer's cap he had bought that afternoon in the yacht-supply shop on the waterfront. He had forgotten how cold a Mediterranean night at sea could be, even in early summer. And here he was practically at sea. Twenty miles out from Naples, at the very tip of the island's breakwater. The *Nessie*'s lights a few hundred yards beyond.

Almost midnight. Had Julia and her party even left Rome yet? He knew those Roman dinners. Endless drinks beginning at nine or ten; then antipasto; then primo, secondo, and on and on, until the exhausted servants poured the sickly finale, the traditional viscous liqueur with its floating coffee beans. The beans were called *mosche,* "flies," most disgusting of all the innumerable Italian symbols of fertility. It was true that among Julia's crowd cognac would probably be substituted.

In any case, wouldn't Julia just insist on a bang-up birthday-eve dinner, instead of being satisfied with the shipboard lunch for which the cooper had told him the *Nessie's* "dining saloon"—she apparently actually called it that—was already decorated. As he cowered beside the cold concrete, a few feet above the dark lapping water, the thought of the lunch gave him hope that the seaplane might arrive soon. For tonight Julia wouldn't want to get to bed too late: she was not one to risk appearing yawning and bedraggled on her birthday.

After the plane's arrival, if he could manage to slip aboard the *Nessie* without being shot, do his little thing with the cooper's promised help, and slip down again with his camera into the water taxi that would be waiting . . . His years as reporter, not to mention some of his other activities, had accustomed him to take chances. So far he'd been lucky. Minor detentions only, like the one the other day in the Commissario's office. Occasional, inevitable disappointments along the line—snubs from proud beauties, like the one from the angelo that same Sunday. Otherwise, a charmed life, if he said so himself. And no great attachment, thank God, no equivalent of a wife; no hanging around mawkish and moping when, more or less fatefully, a connection ended.

A droning sound. The plane? The thicket of stars made it difficult to spy a moving light. But there was new activity on the *Nessie,* or rather beside it, where the smaller mass of the dinghy now showed a glow. Ready to cast off. No headlights yet—lest, he supposed, they blind the pilot. Yes: the drone was louder now; and now much louder; and Lyle could make out the plane's two winking lights, red and green. Suddenly its own great head lamp came on, casting a dazzling path on the water. He saw it hover and circle, its beam carving wheels of light out of the darkness; and now it was skimming the surface, its pontoons leaving parallel phosphorescent trails. When it came to a halt its own headlight was cut; and, bathed in the beam of the approaching dinghy, it became a moth-like silhouette. The dinghy drew close to the plane and held fast; a door swung open; and after a few moments human shadows began to step down from the carapace. Then other human shadows began to hand out baggage, and uplifted arms received it. And then . . .

All he knew was that there was a roar of motors, a sudden glare of floodlights so strong that even he, had anyone been watching, must have been illumined on his distant perch; there were yells, screams, and a volley of shots that made him shrink back into his damp corner. That was followed by another revving of motors and by more shots, this time in two tones as in a duel. The barrage of motors tore the air, diminished, and died away.

Lights had come on in houses along the waterfront; and to his surprise he saw that the boat he had hired to come for him as soon as the plane should land had, despite the shooting, actually set out, and was already halfway toward him across the basin. From the plane and dinghy came a babble of voices, and he saw the dinghy move off, the golden path of its lights brightening the side of the *Nessie.*

In a few moments he was ordering the helmsman of his taxi to steer straight for the yacht. The confusion, whatever its cause, should be to his advantage.

From the dinghy, when Lyle reached it, baggage was being handed up the *Nessie'*s outboard ladder by a quartet of the crew. This was the exact moment the cooper had advised him to arrive; and there was the cooper himself, as promised, standing above him at the rail, taking, or waiting to take, delivery. Saluting, trusting to his new cap and official-looking raincoat, and firmly calling out, "Dogana! Customs!," each word in the strongest Italian accent he could muster, Lyle crossed the dinghy and pushed unchallenged up the steps. On the deck the cooper came toward him. Why was he shaking his head? "Alas!" the cooper said. "There be land-rats and water-rats, land-thieves and water-thieves . . ."

For once, Lyle got the message of the Bard. Everybody knew *that* play. A brief career in his high-school dramatic club had lodged in his mind the terrible word that followed. He gasped. "You mean *Pirates!* You mean—they got Her?"

And it was probably only natural that Security, smarting from its disgrace, should be all the more ferociously on the qui vive. He felt a painful grip on his arm. "Saw you at Swank," said the brute in black leather whose face was only an inch from his own. "You're a friend of that professor friend of Harry's. You wouldn't come aboard when we invited you. How about coming with me to the boss and telling her just what you're doing here now?"

To the boss! Was such bliss *possible?* As a bonus he saw that the gorilla who was clutching him, shoving him, *hurting* him, was really quite handsome in his way.

37

Nat had just fallen asleep when he was wakened by the sound of what in his first consciousness he took to be village fireworks. Quickly realizing what it must be, he went out onto his terrace. Just below him, two shadowy forms stood at their railing. He softly made his presence known, and Sacca called up in the dark: "Professore—you're not afraid of bullets?"

"It's gunfire? Whose is it?"

"Who knows? It's at the harbor. I told you the island was at war."

Words came from the shapeless figure beside Sacca. "The salt war. Yesterday we were told it was settled. And now . . ."

A few more reports, followed by a roar of motors, rose from the marina.

Nat's disingenuous question about the gunfire had been prompted by curiosity as to how much the Saccas knew. Immacolatina would be surprised by how much he himself had learned about the salt war since the evening almost a week ago when she had laughed at his tiny package from Salerno. Sacca's first mention of war had only tangential connection with salt: it referred to the conflict between the Reverend Mother and the Parroco. Standing on his terrace, Nat enjoyed the knowledge, not shared by the Saccas, that neither of those wars was the cause of the present gunfire. He was pleased not because he knew more than they, but because he knew that Ladislao was not involved. Ladislao was sleeping soundly, undisturbed by the shooting.

IT HAD BEEN well after dark the previous evening, and once again Nat had given him up, when Ladislao finally rang the bell of Villa Bklyn. On being asked he admitted to being hungry, and he had much to tell.

Part of it amounted to a revision of Sacca's imaginary item in the Neapolitan press about the encounter between coast guard and spider. Actually, everything about the little black boat, the contraband-runner, had not been "in perfect order." True, it was cargo-less, and it was eventually allowed to continue on its way. But not before the removal of two passengers it was found to be carrying.

Ladislao told about boarding the boat "in a cove at the foot of a cliff. By the time we got there Vispo was using rough language. A man in his position shouldn't have been asked to scramble down a 'goat path' in good clothes—the clothes were mentioned several times. The spider should have been sent to pick him up at the harbor. And so on. He had been 'shown no respect.'" The spidermen—the Consortium's superior servants—barely answered him. And they were careless. As was shown by their forgetting to turn off the signal—"We're empty: stop us if you like"—an omission that resulted in the visit by the law.

In the surprise, Ladislao gave his true name, forgetting that according to his papers—the ones he carried for his work on the island—he was somebody else. (His grimace as he recounted that "mistake" conveyed awareness of its meaning: resignation from the Club.) Vispo lost self-control, Ladislao said. When the coast guardsmen questioned the reason he gave for being on board a spider—"en route to an important conference"—he screamed at them. He'd have them dismissed from the service. The two captives were transferred to one of the cutters and taken to the port and thence to the Commissariato. There the Commissario took the officers aside for a few quiet words. The order for release was quickly given, but Vispo found the accompanying apologies far from adequate.

"So we never did get to the grotto, where I was to have waited and gone out with the spidermen to the seaplane. Vispo wouldn't have come, of course: that was my particular job." Ladislao said his plan had been to let Vispo suppose he had gone with them, but somehow to break away: even, in desperation, if he had actually to board the spider, to slip off as it approached the plane, and swim to shore, probably to the breakwater. How else to have acted in the complexity of the dilemma? After reaching shore he would have improvised some course of action. And indeed improvisation was what faced him now.

They talked until late.

As Nat listened, the figure of Vispo as nephew and half brother emerged in sharper and more cogent detail than Melba had known how, or had chosen, to draw it. Obsession with family was equally, if differently, strong in the two of them: Vispo's had fed on Melba's from the beginning; and her intended beneficence—his exile to Sardinian adoptive parents—had festered. And now there was the new sense of self-importance: the salt assignment by the Consortium had gone to his head, unleashed him, much as the proximity of the picture excited Melba.

" *'Family'!* The word's a nightmare!" (As he said it, Ladislao was unaware that he was echoing a famous Frenchman.) By the passionate cry, he and Nat were both made more conscious of reticence. Ladislao spoke of Vispo, the Club, and in general of his malaise, though not of his recent panic about the nature of his tie to Melba; nor did Nat speak of what Melba had told him of the boy's begetting. But those were islands in the flood of talk between Jason Deming's biographer and the youngest of Deming's descendants.

Recital of the most recent events of all constituted a midnight postscript.

From the police station, Ladislao had accompanied Vispo back to the Imperatore. And there Vispo, already outraged by arrest, was given an even more grievous surprise. In his emergency cancellation of the planned encounter between Clubmen and Nessiemen at Swank he had underestimated the importance of one detail: the presence of the several Consortium officials who had traveled to the island specifically to see the fun. Those personages had not relished their disappointment, and here they were, sitting at one of Mario's tables, their black humor deepened by news they had just heard in the hotel's television room. Against all expectation, despite the best efforts of the Consortium's agents, the state salt refiners had called off their strike. Normal state production of salt was about to resume. Soon the state monopoly itself would end, and salt would be a commodity freely sold throughout Italy. In the interim, the demand for contraband would immediately diminish to its pre-strike trickle. The Consortium's salt campaign, launched to make big and quick profits from the strike, was over. Only one thing seemed to give satisfaction to the disgruntled Consortium gentlemen: their unanimous decision that the services of Signor Vispo would no longer be needed.

There was immediate disagreement over the terms of the

Club's contract. Voices rose. Mario came over and stood by the table; and under cover of the noise, bending down to retrieve a dropped napkin, murmured to Ladislao, like a protective uncle: "Accept the Professor's invitation." The dispute continuing, Ladislao had slipped out. And here he was, at Villa Bklyn.

NAT HAD TO force himself to see in the eager youth beside him that staple of adventure fiction—a threatened man. His description of events had shown him fully aware of the triple danger—Melba's dementia, and the double menace of Vispo and the Nessiemen— and yet in his enthusiasm in talking with this older man about things that touched him immediately and led to wider thoughts, he seemed to forget the pressing circumstances.

"Then Vispo doesn't know where you are?"

"I don't know where he thinks I'll be sleeping tonight. Oh, Professor, you were mentioned. Melba reminded him you once saw Duca slap him."

"She told him that because she's annoyed with me about the picture."

"If I can get her over this crisis she'll be her better self again. Of course I'll always have to watch her."

Did Ladislao really see in a straight clear line, out beyond the threats? What lay along that line? What about Vispo? Toward him he could scarcely feel protective: the watch to be kept there would be of a different kind. Apparently life seemed to him to hold out promises: he spoke of "the future," mentioned a girl he looked forward to seeing "again." But Nat noticed that the promises were not too sharply defined; and he couldn't envisage him, this young escapee from the sordid world he had been drawn into, whole-heartedly ensconced in one of the listed professions. He saw him rather as a non-conformist, something of himself years before. Come to think of it, all the Neapolitan actors in the dramas of the past few days were insurgents, in their different ways: conditions of survival in Naples compelled a desperate ingenuity.

Meanwhile, pending events must be faced.

"The hijacking of the picture is still on, you think? Or off?"

"Probably on. As we left the spider Vispo ordered the men to carry on according to the way he'd sketched the operation to the grotto people over the telephone. The spidermen pretended not to pay him much attention, but he seemed to expect they'd do the job. He knew it would appeal to their arrogance to show they could swing it independently."

Any discussion of "What next?" was precluded by exhaustion: the boy suddenly fell asleep in his chair. Nat woke him to lead him to a couch, where he was immediately again unconscious.

THERE HAD BEEN no shooting for some time; the last yells had died away. Nat saw the side of the *Nessie* briefly illuminated by a head lamp—he supposed the dinghy's. Then the only lights were sparse and faint.

On the terrace below, the two dim forms turned away from the railing. Several hours before, they had seen Ladislao arrive. Now Immacolatina called up, "He is sleeping?" And he heard Sacca say to her, again inconsistent on the subject of entertainment: "The Professore with a houseguest! What an improvement!"

Nat returned to his bed.

Almost before he knew he was there, he was wakened by the pealing of his bell. It was bright daylight; his watch said eight. The bell rang again. Stumbling out, he found at the head of the steps one of the smart bellboys from the Imperatore with a message. Signor Vogel wondered whether he could possibly come to his room at the hotel. An emergency had arisen.

"Signor Vogel?"

"Mr. Harry Vogel, an American. He said you would know his name. Mr. Vogel has to leave the island this morning, and there is something he must talk to you about before he goes."

Ladislao slept on. He had promised to stay close to Villa Bklyn until the *Nessie* departed.

38

As he approached the Imperatore, Nat was passed in the street by the hotel's electric cart, piled with the valises of guests departing on the early hydrofoil. He wondered whether the load included the baggage of Melba and Vispo, and whether he would meet either or both of them, leaving the hotel to rejoin their luggage at the pier. Could Vispo wind up his business on the island so quickly after dismissal? And would Melba be willing to leave without Ladislao, ignorant as she must be of his whereabouts?

But terrace and lobby offered only the spacious fresh emptiness of a big country hotel in the early hours of a sunny summer morning.

In contrast, Mrs. Harry Vogel's voice was shrill over the house phone; and upstairs, in Room 418, Harry, who was limping, pointed to a large, rectangular, flattish carton, torn away on one side. Its content was sufficiently exposed to be, by Nat, instantly recognizable. To his surprise the Vogels, too, knew what it was. "When I went downstairs before breakfast to report what had happened, the concierge was just talking over the telephone in English about the hijacking of one of the Kaloumians' pictures, and it didn't take me long to realize this was the one, so I just asked him to send a boy for you and came right back up here. Who dumped it on us? Why? It's jailbait. Can you imagine any surer jail-bait than a picture probably worth millions belonging to the Kaloumians? Anybody thinks I'm going to turn it in and get locked up by way of thanks, they're crazy."

And Mrs. Harry: "You'd better get us out of this one, *Professor*. You got us into it."

Nat recognized hysteria, and even in his panic Harry came through with a chiding "Now Marge . . . ," adding, in an offended tone, "I think their fuckin' Madonna broke a bone in my foot."

Sometime in the pre-dawn hours, after their return from a local guitar-and-wine cantina with the others, their throats hoarse from joining in "O Sole Mio," a banging on the door had wakened them. Harry had run barefoot to open it, and before he could jump back the heavy carton had fallen into the room "like something alive," and "got him on the instep." By the time he'd peered out, the corridor was empty.

Nat had no doubt that the number of either Melba's or Vispo's room would be found to bear a mistakable resemblance to 418; and it was probably just as well that the hall had been empty— that Harry didn't have to wonder whether, full of wine, sleep and "O Sole Mio," he had really glimpsed, or only imagined, a fleeing figure in fancy dress, perhaps wearing a red bandanna and gold earrings. He'd had the sense to forbid Marge to say a word to their friends. "I sent for you as soon as I could because you're the only person we know in this hellhole. What do we do now?" The Vogels' agitation was perhaps excusable. First, their boat had been practically sunk under them. Now, an illicit Old Master had been thrown at, or on, their feet. Given the predictable all-out scramble by Italian, or perhaps international, police to gain the glory of retrieving the Kaloumians' instantly famous Madonna, the ordeal facing anyone who might deliver the carton to the authorities scarcely bore thinking about. It should be got at once to the *Nessie*, and the *Nessie* was less than a thousand yards away. But how to transport it?

"You have your leatherman friend," Nat reminded Harry. "You couldn't get in touch with him and have him take the picture to the yacht? No, I suppose not: to protect himself he'd have to tell where he got it, so that wouldn't work."

"You're damn right it wouldn't. And who says he's a friend? Who'd trust him after that treatment yesterday?"

It had taken a little time for the full indignity of the guided tour of the *Nessie* to sink into the sextet's collective sensibility. Now it was rankling. "We all agreed last night," Harry said, "to try not to be bitter about what's happened on this trip—the crook skipper, and Hickey having the gall to turn us over to those gunmen. Not to mention a few other things, more personal, like that chunk of steak in Salerno, and now my instep. We've got to remember we've met some very wonderful warm people over here, especially that fellow, what's his name, the one with the long nose, that took charge when our stuff went down the drink and got us put up here and had the Princess do the shopping. And you too, Sir, that is if you can help us lick this latest problem."

"Sir"! It had the effect of making him—was perhaps meant to make him—feel once again, as he had with the sextet in the piazza, like the shepherd of a flock, responsible now, as Marge had decreed, for solving the dilemma. The picture should be got to its chapel, and in such a way that no news of its vicissitudes would reach Melba or Ladislao: the sooner and the more quietly its journey ended, the better for everybody, but especially for them. He could think of only one possible way.

"How much time before your hydrofoil?"

"We're scheduled for the ten o'clock, to pick up tickets in Naples for the . . ."

"The plane to Rome! And then the plane home! Thank God! *On Wis-con-sin . . . !*" Marge did a little joy-dance.

"Wait here," Nat ordered.

Downstairs he was luckier than he expected. Mario, seldom on duty before noon, was already on his terrace, though unfamiliar in sport shirt and slacks. He responded to Nat's beckoning: "I've come early this morning, Professore, because . . ."

With sufficient apology Nat was able to postpone the explanation, substitute a quiet one of his own, ask a few questions, and move to an inconspicuous corner to wait.

Mario's apparently casual chat with the concierge lasted several minutes, and he walked slowly back. "Signor Vispo is in Room 408. Departure by ten o'clock hydrofoil. Yes: it is known that a person such as you describe was seen to bring in a large parcel late last night. It is not known to what room or even what floor he delivered it: no one in his right mind would risk challenging a member of that particular group. But you are right: eventually someone on the staff will talk, has perhaps talked already. The police are bound to come. Outgoing luggage is certainly being checked at the pier."

Back in Room 418 Nat said: "Get out of the hotel now. Immediately. I'll stay here. Get hold of the others and all leave together. The hotel will have you taken to the hydrofoil. If you see anybody on the dock or on board you've seen before, say no more than hello. Just get off the island and on your way. Forget you've ever seen the picture or heard of it. Still no mention of it to the others."

Thanks and fervent invitations to visit M'waukee streamed back from the hastily obedient pair—they had no luggage to delay them—as he stood at the door and watched them go.

The carton was soon out of sight behind a curtain.

After a few minutes a maid, alerted from below, came as he had expected to check the room—count bottles in the refrigerator, discover whether departing guests had forgotten diamonds or removed segments of the decor. Recognition of him as former guest and island inhabitant assured her smiling compassion for the not uncommon predicament he confessed to: sudden mal di stomaco while saluting his friends; what to do but stay behind until the emergency passed? When she had gone, he resumed his watch at the door.

It was the custom in the island's better hotels for the luggage of all guests leaving by the same hydrofoil to be collected from their rooms and transported en masse to the dock, where each owner claimed his pieces before boarding. Any minute now the luggage of Room 408 should be called for, and there was a chance that the carton could be deftly added to it, for discovery at the pier. Or, if that proved impossible, it could perhaps be slipped into 408 immediately following Vispo's departure. By whichever route, it would eventually be delivered to the *Nessie* via the police. With luck it could result in Vispo's apprehension and temporary removal from circulation. From what Ladislao had said, it seemed unlikely that the Consortium would spring to his aid.

As he stood looking toward the door of 408 Nat wondered what Vispo would have done with the carton had it reached him that night. Taken it through the empty halls to Melba's room, he supposed, and leaned it against her door as he would have found it leaning against his; perhaps roused her as he had been roused; and certainly fled—leaving her to the crazy ecstasy of discovery and repossession. Until . . .

What, after that, would have been Melba's fate?

A hotel porter came into view from the corridor's opposite end. Walking slowly, empty-handed, past what must be 402, 404, 406. Bad sign that he wasn't pushing a luggage cart. But yes: he knocked at 408. He disappeared within. And came out again: but carrying only a single case, with which he walked easily away and was gone.

The hope of adding picture to luggage was dashed. The watch resumed.

How long would Melba have enjoyed the recaptured prize? Some time during the morning, had she stayed in her room, there would have been a ring, a polite request from the management to be allowed to visit; or, more brutally, the Carabinieri themselves would have rapped on the door. It was difficult to picture Melba in the subsequent circumstances. Nor did he want to. She had invited her ruin, but that made it no more pleasant to imagine. And

Ladislao? He would certainly have offered himself up, claimed responsibility: had it not been for him, his aunt would not have known of the picture's proximity.

Vispo! Emerging from 408. Hesitating in the doorway. Standing there, unzipping his briefcase, looking inside it—some last-minute uncertainty. How sour he looked! That beak of his was longer than ever—sharp as a weapon. Outlined by a long crease down each side before the cheek began. God make him leave the door open! Departing guests often did so: no reason to close the door of an emptied room. Coming out, now. But drawing the door to, behind him. Not all the way, please! Be careless! Now he was in the hall. Nat had heard no click. Vispo was walking away, turning the corner toward the lift. There was the risk that some second thought might bring him back, but Nat had to act now, before the maid came. While the hall was still empty.

He half-carried, half-dragged, the heavy carton. He heard the lift door open and close. Vispo was gone. And the door of 408 was ajar.

Somebody whistling, approaching. Someone had come *up* in the lift! Quick! Push the door open! The clumsy carton, caught on the doorjamb! Too late! Somebody coming into view, around the corner. A man . . .

He'd forgotten who else was staying at the Imperatore.

"Lyle!" Unshaved, wearing a yachtsman's cap, carrying a raincoat.

"Nat! For God's sake! *What have you got there?*"

39

As he had suspected he might, Lyle had suffered some unpleasantness following his apprehension aboard the *Nessie*. The triumph of being ushered into Julia's boudoir had its price. He found her magnificent, a lioness as always, today attended by handmaidens. That is, gathered round her were the guests whose silhouettes he had seen leaving the seaplane; all were women. Lyle recognized them immediately—as who in his world would not? The much-photographed, ostentatiously Westernized wives of half a dozen Middle-Eastern potentates, viceroys in L.K.'s empire. Their presence here meant that somewhere a conference was in progress, following which L.K. would bring his six emirs by flying carpet for the douceur of a *Nessie* cruise. Meanwhile, despite extravagant and competitive chic, each was suffering the inevitable fate of her sex in Julia's presence: eclipse. Beside Julia, what woman had ever felt herself refulgent? And with joyful heart Lyle saw that among these exotics Julia was already bored—bored as any corporation president's lady stuck with half a dozen suburban vice-presidential wives.

It was one of Julia's specialties never to show surprise, and as the gorilla all but threw Lyle into the room she glanced up and coolly said: "Ladies, I think you must all know my notorious cousin, Lyle Brennan," setting off the characteristic murmur evoked by the appearance of a media celebrity. She let them think what they liked about his mode of entrance. Then she serenely excused herself and asked Lyle to step outside with her.

The next few minutes called for the greatest patience, with

the gorillas crowding close in the narrow passage between the rows of cabins and relishing every bit of the invective Julia spat at him.

As cousin, Lyle had long experience with the family tongue: and had he wished, could have given as good as he got. But today he did not wish. When Julia's litany finally ended he knew enough to ignore those large segments which had been general or retrospective. He replied only to her closing aspersion. Namely, that knowing his capacity for enormities as she unfortunately did, it should have occurred to her from the first, even before he so brazenly flaunted himself into her presence that night of all nights, that only he of all so-called human beings could possibly be responsible for what she chose to call "the rape of my Virgin Mary."

That brought a growl from the retainers. But Lyle thought fast, and from two of them he succeeded in extracting grudging confirmation that he had been at Swank not only simultaneously with, but actually in the company of, a certain Princess and her nephew. Later, he had seen that pair again, separately, and learned of their previous ownership of the picture and their continued obsession with it. To these obvious suspects he could lead the police; and it was precisely to offer his cousin such assistance that he had made his way, in the dark and under fire, to the *Nessie*. "My boatman is waiting right now, alongside, to take me back," he said stoutly, as though that were proof of something.

Julia gave him one of the long level looks that were another of her stocks in trade. "Send the boatman away, somebody," she ordered. "My cousin will be spending the night on board. He speaks Italian. He can help me with the next round of this boring business."

"My dears, I almost aborted out of pure relief and gratitude" was the way Lyle later described that moment to chosen intimates as they sat round in or out of caftans beside the pool at his villa near Venice.

Already the telephone could be heard ringing inside the

boudoir, and he could picture the flurry of the exotics, wondering whether or not to answer. And indeed one of them half-opened the door, stuck out her overcoiffed head, and said "Telephone!" in an ingratiating way that made him and Julia seek each other's bright green eyes to enjoy together such a moment as they had often shared in the past.

That was L.K. on the line, from Rome. He had already alerted "everybody"; and much of the rest of the night, after the guests had been sent to bed, was spent answering resultant Roman calls. Rome suspected that the picture had already left the island; nevertheless Rome had ordered the island police to take the primary precaution of checking the ferries; Rome had alerted Naples. Rome had already wakened the art dealer and sent someone to fetch a photograph of the picture which in a few hours would become known around the world—its previous provenance forgotten—as "the Kaloumian Madonna." And in the morning Roman detectives and a television crew would fly to the *Nessie.*

During the intervals between the calls, Lyle was finding Julia mellower. Champagne was brought in; that helped. She told him that she had joined the *Nessie* at the island instead of at Naples because of a recent Neapolitan episode involving the holdup of some of the crew. "L.K. always encourages the boys to familiarize themselves with the customs of the country, and here in Italy they've been into something local connected with salt." The Neapolitan holdup had involved the temporary disappearance of an American colonel and total disappearance of the colonel's car. Altogether, Naples sounded like a place where "anyone's Madonna might be kidnapped, let alone ours"; therefore better avoided, in favor of the island. "Appointment in Samarra!" they simultaneously cried; and the reminder of how much each of them had always been the other's kind of person soon had them giggling about the kidnapping of a colonel and agreeing that most colonels they'd known deserved no better fate. Before long Lyle felt they were almost back on old terms. It was decided that in the early morning the dinghy would take him ashore and wait while he freshened up at the hotel. Then, when the men from Rome arrived, he would tell them what he knew.

However, as they separated to get a few hours sleep, Julia gave him another of her long looks, smiling slightly. He knew what it meant. Even if by some miracle he were to find the Madonna himself, and deliver it to her personally, on his knees—perhaps *especially* in that case—her suspicions of him as the engineer of the theft would forever remain. There was some pride to be taken from that thought. Suspicion from Julia was a tribute: cousin found worthy of cousin.

And the show! It promised now to be spectacular, whether the Madonna surfaced or not.

"WHAT HAVE I got here? You can see what it is, Lyle. You saw the photograph."

"This is *IT!*"

"Wish it weren't. Trying to get rid of it."

"Rid of it *here?*"

"Leaving it here so it will be found and reach the *Nessie.*"

"The *Nessie!* I'll take it there myself!"

"Sh! There's the maid. Help me shove it into the room and close the door on it."

"Certainly not. It stays with me."

And in a flash it was covered by Lyle's raincoat, which had as though fallen to the floor between them.

The maid smiled at them both. "Feeling better, Professore?"

"Still not quite ready to go out. Mr. Brennan's taking me to his room."

"Rice, Professore. Rice with oil. And if that doesn't work, boiled onions."

She entered 408 and was quickly out again, shutting the door behind her. She bade them farewell.

As soon as she disappeared Nat tried the doorknob and swore. "Now what do we do with it?"

"I'll take it straight to Julia, of course."

"Julia has arrived?"

"She has."

"You've seen her?"

"I have."

"How did it go?"

"Perfectly."

Lyle's extreme crispness, born of excitement and caution, brought from Nat a look of curiosity, and an end to questions. "There's a gauntlet to be run between here and the *Nessie*, you know," Nat said, "what with everybody in and out of the hotel undoubtedly alerted by now. We need more around this thing than just the raincoat. Disguising the shape, we may get it to a water taxi unchallenged."

"No need to hire a boat. The dinghy's at the pier, awaiting my orders. Did you say *'we'*?"

"I said *'we.'* "

"I say *'I.'* "

"It's *'we,'* I'm afraid. You're giving me an unexpected chance to witness actual delivery to the *Nessie,* and for good reasons I'm jumping at it. You can see we're dependent on each other. I can't possibly get the picture to the yacht on my own, and you can't deliver it without me, because if you tried I could have you pinched on the way. From what you've told me about your cousin, I suspect she'd enjoy that. So pipe down. I'll come along, see the picture aboard, and disappear, leaving you in full sequel. Okay?"

Lyle couldn't accept with good grace, but he accepted. He could afford to placate the poor psychographer, whose mention of "sequel" revealed the envy of a have-not. ("De haut en bas," as he later put it to the caftan set around his pool.) Together they took the carton, draped in the raincoat, to Lyle's room. Lyle consented to the use of most of his wardrobe, painful though it was to see some of the silk creations contorted into rags. Nat telephoned to the chief barman—why him?—for some heavy cord, and strangely enough the chief barman brought it himself. Nat showed him the now shapeless bundle. "Mario, Mr. Brennan is contributing some clothes he doesn't need to the hospice, the old people's home on the road down to the port. Rather unsightly, as you see. Will the hotel object if we take it out through the lobby and the front door?"

Mario considered. "To take something that size as far as the ospizio you'll be wanting a taxi. At the front, the bellboys would expect to relieve you of the parcel, to carry it to the taxi rank themselves or call a porter. If you'd rather do it all yourselves, I suggest the service door."

He helped them with the tying and took them down the back lift. At the small door opening out into a lane he murmured, "Just follow the garden wall"; and more loudly, since staff were coming and going around the time clock, ". . . and you'll reach the ospizio."

MADDENING, Lyle found it, after those precautions, that when they had gone only a few yards there should appear from around a corner the most unwelcome person conceivable. It was like a rerun of his own turning the corner of the hotel corridor half an hour before, when Nat was trying to push the carton into the room. His own face must at that moment have displayed this same surprise, followed by this same astonished comprehension. The boy was even unshaved, like himself, and his words were almost exactly what his own had been: *"Professor: what have you got there?"*

And Nat told him, for Christ's sake. He didn't name it; but in a low, stern voice he told him: "We agreed it was essential for you to keep clear. In a few minutes it will be where it belongs, and you can forget it. Where are you going?"

"I wanted to see Melba before she leaves. I wanted to make sure it hadn't reached her, or try to do something if it had. The back door is best for me here. Did you get it from her?"

"It hasn't been anywhere near her."

"Thank God for that. Then how . . . ?"

"Forget it, Ladislao. Since you didn't stay where you promised, yes, go to Melba. I'll join you there. This errand shouldn't take long."

"Why do you have to go with it, Professor?"

That, at least, Lyle thought, was a good question, though accompanied by a look in his direction that one couldn't exactly enjoy.

"I want to be sure it arrives on board and the story's over."

"So do I. It's what I want more than anything. I'll come too."

"Absolutely not. You must do nothing of the kind. We're taking it to the dinghy. *The dinghy.*"

"I'm coming, Professor. It means more to me than it does to you."

"Perhaps. But you must let me do it."

There was a moment of silence.

Lyle had been finding the conversation difficult to follow. Nat and the boy had been talking in riddles. He knew from the brief meeting in the street the day before, when he and the cooper had been hissed at from an alley, that for some reason the dukeling wanted to keep the picture away from his aunt, the old principessa. That, of course, was all to the good. But now something else was looming. In addition to Nat, the boy too was eager to horn in on his—Lyle's own—sequel. Lyle had been hoping that once beside the dinghy there might even be some way· of ditching Nat. Perhaps a pair would be easier to dump than one.

"Go to Melba, and wait for me there."

The boy stood a moment longer, then without further word continued past them. Nat stared after him, to see him enter the hotel.

BUT HE MUST HAVE gone to the funicular, instead, for he was down at the port before them.

After directing the taxi driver to the hospice in a voice that others might hear, when they were on their way Nat told him to continue to the water's edge. There, from the taxi they spotted the boy on the fringe of a group of idlers gathered to stare at the dinghy. But he himself was looking landward, watching for their arrival. Nat's face turned grim. "For God's sake pay him no attention, Lyle. He mustn't be noticed."

"I have no wish to notice him, I assure you."

They paid the taxi, extracted the bundle, carried it together to the water stairs at whose foot the dinghy was waiting. "Permesso, permesso." Onlookers lining the seawall separated to let them through.

The helmsman in black looked up. Lyle greeted him. "I'm ready. My friend here seems to be coming too. Give us a hand with this, will you? Careful: it's something precious for Mrs. K."

Down the slippery steps. The bundle handed over. It and they in the dinghy. Nat was proving unditchable, but the boy, at least, watching them from the wall, was making no move. "Can't we get going?"

"Hickey's just coming down the quay now, Mr. Brennan. We'll wait for him, if you don't object." Nat had just time to register the insolence, when the helmsman began to roar. "Pat! There's that fucker from the convent, standin' there gawpin' at us! Get hold of him, will y'? I'm comin'!"

Not every one of the islanders watching from the seawall saw every detail, but every detail had its witnesses.

Many saw the helmsman scramble out of the boat and up the steps, fast followed by the quiet Professore who had been living at Villa Bklyn; and saw the Professore lose his footing on the oily stairs and fall backward into the water. While that was happening, others in the crowd were thudded into, spun round, knocked down by the second leatherman as he cannoned through them toward a young man standing at the edge of the wall—a young man only a

200

few had ever seen before. The leatherman raised an arm to strike. Before the blow fell they heard the young man call out, and saw him dive into the water near where the Professore had gone under. Silence instantly fell over the onlookers, and lasted a long minute. Then the two men surfaced, one after the other; and the Carabiniere on waterfront duty that morning ran over to the scene of shouting and cheering.

NAT'S PANIC under the water was due not so much to the gagging—and he seemed to be gagging less on water than on garbage (it brought him a mad thought of Harry the choker and his chunk of steak)—as to the knowledge that one of his feet was caught by what he supposed must be a mooring rope or anchor chain. Nevertheless, when in the darkness he felt his foot suddenly released he knew it was just in time: his lungs wouldn't have held out much longer. As he surfaced, he retched and spewed up—narrowly missing Ladislao's face, which had just emerged from the turbid harbor water barely a yard from his own. The astonishing thing was that in the next moment their eyes met and they laughed.

Arms hoisted Nat out onto the steps, and he sat there streaming and hunched over. Breathing was painful, as if his thorax had caved in. He saw Ladislao wave away offers of help and lift himself easily onto the step above him. Raising his eyes, he became aware of an enormity: the two leathermen had jumped back into the dinghy and were preparing to cast off, urged on by agitated words and gestures from Lyle. Rage gave strength: and Nat, still heaving and speechless, was able to turn and in frantic sign language induce spectators to attract the Carabiniere's attention. Witnesses of the assault must have supplied the officer with convincing testimony, for seeing the hit-and-run intent he acted at once, shouting to the dinghy, and, when that had no immediate effect, firing a shot into the air. Nat saw the automatic reaction—the instant plunging of two right hands inside two bulging black jackets—and then saw the exchange of glances, the shrugs, and the hands withdrawn empty: probably even *Nessie* house rules discouraged outright gun duels with the law. The Carabiniere's shot brought one of his colleagues running from the barracks on the quay, and the first descended the steps and asked Nat, amid the noise of the crowd, whether he wished to be taken to the hospital.

Testing his power to reply, he found he could croak: "No, thank you."

"Do you want these men arrested?"

"Not now. Tell them to take us to the yacht." He forced the words out, wanting Lyle to hear. "And please come with us, Maresciallo." Even in his present state he didn't forget the oral promotion one accords, in Italy, as elsewhere, when addressing the rank and file of the force.

In a moment the load of them, Lyle the picture of resentment, the leathermen expressionless, were crossing the harbor toward the breakwater and the *Nessie.* From the crowd on the pier came colorful imprecations. The policeman's gun was back in its holster, his hand not far from it. Ladislao's face was streaked with oil, his hair festooned with rubbish. Nat supposed he must look the same. They sat there soggy and wordless. As they rounded the breakwater, Nat saw a seaplane resting on the water close to the yacht. The plane of last night, he supposed. But hadn't they just passed that very plane, berthed at a jetty, inside the harbor? What was this—a second seaplane, or an illusion? He was still confused after his trip to the bottom.

40

THANKS TO the policeman's presence, Nat could without trouble ensure that it was he and Ladislao, and no one else, who actually delivered the bundle to the *Nessie:* together they lifted it up the ladder. In the dinghy Nat had seen the leatherman Hickey murmur into his walkie-talkie; no surprise, then, that the same two white-jacketed "guides" were waiting on deck. Nat ignored them. Lyle's humor had for some reason noticeably improved: even Nat's cool "Will you tell your cousin we're here?" seemed not to offend him. His questioning glance toward the stewards, however, the stony look they returned, the aggressiveness with which one of them put himself forward as escort, reinforced Nat's impression, first derived from the helmsman's words in the dinghy, that Lyle Brennan's reconciliation with Cousin Julia had yet to become, at least in the eyes of her private army, a completely established fact. Lyle went off with his guard.

As Nat and Ladislao waited on deck, dripping and bedraggled—"two wet sea boys," the cooper might have called them— watching their bundle, themselves closely watched by the second steward, who was in turn watched by the policeman, they exchanged their first words since immersion. Each had leaped to save the other; there had been no need, as there had been no chance, for comment. With their leaps, the twenty-four hours of acquaintance had leaped also—into friendship; and that too they both knew.

"Vispo left the hotel. You don't suppose Melba went with him?"

"She didn't. I phoned her room as I passed through the lobby. I told her to wait."

"How did she sound?"

"Better, I thought. I hope."

"Any ideas as to what you'll do?"

"Only that there's one thing we can't do—go back to the palazzo, at least just now."

The first steward was back, alone, holding a door open. "Okay, Professor, this way." They took up their bundle, and Nat signaled to the policeman to follow.

As they passed through one of the salons, Nat caught sight of the two of them in a large mirror, and was fully aware for the first time of the deplorable spectacle they presented.

"Follow me, please."

They descended a flight of stairs into a region that had not been included in the guided tour, and reached a door marked "Swimming Pool." Their guide stopped. "Wait here, please." And entered, closing the door behind him.

The door opened. "Come in, please."

THE SIGHT OF the second seaplane had told Lyle that the detectives and television men from Rome had arrived; and from that moment he had utter confidence in the show that would be his sequel. It would of course bear the scar of Nat's interference; but already he saw how that scar could be transformed into an adornment. The essential was the logic of the tapes. Whatever tapes the people from Rome might make, he and Julia would be on them. Being Italian products, the tapes would be his for the asking (the dollar still counted for something); and though Julia might say beastly things, and Nat might be honored, tapes were now famous— presidentially famous—for being easily alterable.

Julia's beastliness—her unspeakableness that one could only admire—began at once, the moment the steward ushered Lyle into the area of the *Nessie*'s swimming pool, where the odalisques in bright beach robes were sitting with her at breakfast—a breakfast which, he could see, the men from Rome (there were about a dozen of them) had also been invited to share. Assorted servants stood about. Discussion of the hijacking could only have begun, and he hoped that he might have the space of a few seconds in which to proclaim to the assembly that he, Lyle Brennan, had FOUND the lost Madonna, found her standing in the hallway of his hotel: such an announcement would certainly impress everybody except Julia. But trust Julia to get ahead of him. "Well, Lyle, I suppose you found it?" was her welcome before he could open his mouth. "You did? I was sure you would. This is my cousin," she announced to those who didn't know. And added a few words that didn't totally displease him, testifying as they did again to a certain reciprocity of cousinly admiration: "He has his own way of finding things." And then: *"Where is it, Lyle?"*

Already, quickly moving technicians had turned on lights and mike; already he was on camera with Julia.

When he said that the Madonna was on the deck of this very yacht, where he had arranged her delivery by none other than the young Duca (so Lyle, if not the *Libro d'oro,* ennobled Ladislao) whose family had once owned the collection, and "an American professor who wrote about its founder," Julia calmly and infuriatingly rejoined: "But that must be Nathaniel Haley. I have his book beside my bed. One of the little curators in my museum gave it to me when I said I wanted to be sure I was buying a genuine picture for myself just for once. It reassured me completely. A very *rare* book. An enormously *distinguished* book." Julia the intellectual rides again. She ordered that Professor Haley and the Duca be escorted to her presence at once; and: "Bring me the copy of *Jason Deming* that's in my cabin." Before long the Professor and the Duca were announced, and the lights—this was Lyle's suggestion—were turned full on the door.

Lyle hadn't been sure until Nat and the boy actually entered the pool area that the steward, after accepting the tip he had time to slip him, would honor his promise to "bring them in as they are, exactly as they are." If the two of them, Nat especially, insisted on barging in on somebody else's sequel, then let them appear, and be forever recorded in the media, as the two all-but-drowned rats— rats in every sense of the word—they were. But, as they came through the door, applause and cries of welcome rang out from Julia and her guests and the others. All of it for the two drowned rats and the bundle they were carrying.

Thereafter, Lyle found himself merely one of the group watching Nat being televised shaking hands with Julia, bowing to the company, presenting his revolting little soi-disant ducal side- kick. It was maddening to observe that, on camera and in context, the unkempt, drenched condition of the unspeakable pair made them look not ridiculous, as he had hoped, but like heroes who had suffered in a good cause; and when the Madonna was unwrapped, bringing more applause as she emerged from her cocoon, there was a moment of bitterness as he reflected what the colorful layers of silk protection, now heedlessly discarded, actually were. Julia thanked Nat—of course seeking out Lyle to give him one of her smiles as she did so—for being the Madonna's recoverer. She asked him, while she and he were still on camera, to autograph his great book, his brilliant, his best-selling book—"my *favorite* book"; and as everyone applauded yet again, mike and lights were turned off.

Lyle could tolerate it only because he knew that out of it he could make a sensational show. Incomparably better than the pallid substitute he had almost been willing to settle for—the version whose abortion had resulted in his being dragged before Julia. And if, as he hoped, he was invited to the birthday lunch, there might be additional trimmings. The whole thing would be held together and spiced up by the interview with the cooper, to be done in New York, about contrasting backstairs life aboard the *Nessie*.

PERHAPS BECAUSE he had been weakened by his underwater ordeal, Nat was soon fatigued by the burden of Mrs. Kaloumian's attention, the fleshly reality of her Becky Sharp expression, long familiar from photographs, her caressing voice; and longed to get away. When one thought of her as the Deming Madonna rediviva she was positively frightening. Even though he said forthrightly that now he and Ladislao had better go, he thought his words sounded a little like those of a loyal subject asking royalty's permission to withdraw. No doubt the legend was at work. This Queen and Empress put her soft hand on his. "A reward was offered, you know. To whom shall I have it sent?"

"I'll spell the name for you."

She beckoned to her secretary. Nat spelled. As though inspecting a possible acquisition, Mrs. Kaloumian then looked over toward the disheveled Ladislao, who was keeping well in the background. "My God, he looks like Leslie Howard and doesn't use his title?" The choice of matinee idol dated her, and for a moment Nat could picture an innocent little Julia Brennan—wide-eyed in more ways than one—being taken in her velvet frock to an afternoon showing of *The Scarlet Pimpernel.*

"The address," Nat said, "should be in care of me." There was rich, rippling laughter as she heard the name of the villa.

She was arranging for the dinghy to take them ashore when there was an interruption. The chief of the detectives, accompanied by the Carabiniere. Now that the picture was back, it was normal that there should be no official interest expressed in who had hijacked it. That was the Italian, perhaps the universal, way of justice. The detective's concern was about something else. "Signora—my colleague here has been telling me about an incident at the pier. Considerable local indignation. He thinks a police boat might well come to question members of your crew. . . . Certainly highly inadvisable that any of them go ashore. . . . Indeed, suggest for your own greater comfort that you immediately move the yacht to other waters. . . . We shall now go along ourselves. . . ."

There followed much hasty movement around the swimming pool.

Up on deck the cooper, who had been a silent, service member of the pool party, brought out the ship's bullhorn, which he assured Nat could do everything but wake the dead; and Nat's last memory of the *Nessie* was the cooper's wasting what might have been a tremendous magnification of moanings from the platform at Elsinore, or the keenings of withered witches, on: "TAXI-I-I! TAXI-I-I!"—bawled toward the waterfront.

The dinghy ferried the Romans to their seaplane; and when the small boat came for those going ashore—Lyle was not among them—Nat was surprised to find the party joined by the cooper himself, carrying a suitcase. "I thought," Nat said, "that Lyle was threatening to fly you to New York."

"Yes, Professor, there was indeed a question of my venturing to the brave new world. But I gather you didn't overhear, as I did, the little interchange between Mrs. K. and the head of the television crew? She had him sign a paper she dictated to her secretary, agreeing not to sell or rent or give away or dispose of in any manner any of the tapes that were made today, without her express permission. Since that's the very material Mr. Brennan's counting on for the show I was to be part of, and since I've heard Mrs. K. on the subject of Mr. B., I thought I wouldn't wait for Mr. B. to tell me I'm not needed. I liked the island yesterday—the climate's delicate, the air most sweet—I've got a little cash saved—I decided to jump ship and enjoy things for a while."

Nat reflected that, not counting the policeman (who might have his own eccentricities), the little water taxi was carrying a trio of oddballs.

41

N<small>AT WAS SURPRISED</small> to hear the village clock strike only eleven as he climbed the stairs of Villa Bklyn; and further indication of how short the memorable morning had been was provided by Sacca's start at his disarray: even the island's rampant grapevine hadn't yet transmitted news of the incident at the pier. Nat said merely that he had "got wet"; and Sacca didn't press for details, being impatient to give news of his own.

"Professore! I imagine you haven't heard the carillon today?"

Full as he was of the morning's events, Nat needed a moment to focus his thought. "No, now that you mention it I haven't heard it, I think."

"That's because Fedora has won, Professore! Fedora has won!"

Again Nat had to concentrate. Fedora? Oh, yes: the Reverend Mother, and her feud with the Parroco.

"There has been a settlement, Professore. We'll not be hearing the carillon for a while. And the convent is to share in the church collections after all."

"How did your wonderful cousin accomplish that?" It was a morning for wonderful cousins.

Sacca rolled his eyes, laid a forefinger beside his nose, and said something Nat didn't fully understand about the priest's choosing to keep from the Archbishop any mention of having celebrated from the churchtop a birthday that had turned out to be his own. "A little later," Sacca said, "Fedora may let him play his music box from time to time, if he's a good boy."

Nat congratulated him; but he was too preoccupied to

give much thought to the striding nun and her victory.

He heard more about her later in the day. Ladislao, who had gone directly from the water taxi to Melba, arrived at Villa Bklyn toward the end of the afternoon. He reported finding his aunt "subdued, depressed, a little vague": a reaction stronger than usual, but proportionate to what had been the extraordinary excitement. "She went along very calmly with Reverend Mother and me," Ladislao said. "As though the move was only what she had been expecting all along."

"The move?"

The boy put his hand to his head. "So much has been happening. I was assuming you'd already heard. Reverend Mother learned about Melba's staying on the island after Vispo left, and came to offer her a room in the convent. She said she owed her at least that much. What for, I didn't quite gather from either of them. We moved Melba from the Imperatore right away. I thought she might rest in the convent for a few days and I'd keep an eye on her from here, if you don't mind."

WHEN SEVERAL DAYS had passed, Ladislao telephoned the porter at Palazzo Rovigliano and learned that the Club had decamped. The jukebox and other furniture had been removed by night, the room left open and empty. "The telephone rings once in a while, Don Ladì, but not very often." Nothing had been heard of Vispo.

"We could try going back now, I suppose," Ladislao said to Nat. "But Melba seems to have taken an aversion to the palazzo. And she worries about me. I can see why, but she shouldn't. There's just one thing for me to do—go back to the city and find some work. Almost anything, for the time being. Until I sort things out."

Nat said nothing.

That same evening, in a restaurant, they heard a familiar voice from a nearby table: the cooper, standing, wearing a splashed and spotted apron, was discussing the menu with a group of English. When he had finished he came over. "I was called out of the kitchen to translate," he said. And: "I've found myself a nice little local friend. Cousins of hers own this place, and they gave me this dinner job washing dishes. During the day I enjoy the island with her. Sounds and sweet airs that give delight. A lovely life. It won't last, I suppose. Somebody from home with the right connections is bound to turn up and find me just too valuable to leave behind."

Nat wondered, when the cooper left them, whether Ladislao's thoughts at the moment were, as so often, similar to his own; Ladislao was perhaps not destined to become the Establishment's stoutest pillar, but he was no strolling player, either. Perhaps he was wishing he were.

ONE MORNING there arrived Mrs. Kaloumian's check—or rather a check signed by the treasurer of a corporation with an international-sounding name and marked "Special Services." When Nat finally convinced Ladislao, with avuncular Neapolitan logic, that it was properly his—it would keep him going for a year or two—the boy took Melba to Naples, "for the day." A week went by without word; then Nat had a note from Melba asking him to visit her here on the island at the convent.

She was waiting for him in the parlor. It was his first sight of her since their cool parting: the recent excitement had aged her. His disgrace was apparently forgotten, and indeed as they talked he had the impression that she found it easy to efface whole chunks of the past. From Naples she had returned to the island alone, after taking what she wanted from the palazzo and closing its door behind her "forever." "I used the occasion to reply to my sister-in-law and thank her for letting Laddie and me stay there all these years. I must always remember that it was kind of her to do that. If she had put us out, I don't know where we'd have gone."

There was no mention of the picture, whose photograph in the clipping from the Great Lakes newspaper could have been the only reason for "replying" to the Duchess. It occurred to Nat that if the Duchess had obliged aunt and nephew to leave the palazzo there would have been no renting to the Club, so rich in consequences. But perhaps Vispo would have found his way, inexorably, to Melba and Ladislao wherever they were.

"Still no news of Vispo?"

"No."

She was now "in residence," as she put it, at the convent. No question of joining the order: too late for that, even if she had wanted to. But invited to be a permanent boarder. She referred vaguely to "Fedora's recognition of certain obligations." Refuge for the rest of her days was ensured by that "recognition," plus her own savings. These had proved to be somewhat more substantial than she remembered, and Laddie had said she must now use them entirely for herself. (It obviously hadn't occurred to her that he might have added to the bank account.)

"And Ladislao?"

There was a pause: Melba must have recalled, willy-nilly, some of their earlier talk about the boy. Her hesitation was the more memorable because it was followed by adulation—a torrent, a litany to Laddie's goodness, his devotion, his blessedness—and by protestations of her own measureless love. To the Professor, Laddie had sent a word: "Arrivederci"—a message Nat felt confidence in. Laddie was living in the palazzo "for the time being"; he was "making plans"—she didn't know what they were or whether he expected to return to the university. He would visit her on the island when he could.

"It is right that he should come to see me here. His mother was from this island."

"Oh?" Nat had never, of course, been told who Ladislao's mother was.

"More appropriate than Palazzo Rovigliano. That will never be his, you know. He stands no chance to inherit. He isn't a Rovigliano."

The bad old record, back on the machine. The evil born of

excluding a bastard from "the family" could never have been more blatantly evident than in the story of Vispo; yet Melba could talk this way even of her other nephew, the boy she claimed to adore. "Your brother did his best to recognize him, Melba. And even if he hadn't, he'd still be your brother's son."

"No. No. Laddie is not my brother's son. I just said: he isn't a Rovigliano. I remember what I told you—that Riccardo found the right person and begot a son, and that I was present at the birth, and that I brought Laddie up. But Laddie was not that child. That child died almost at once. There was no telling my brother, so enchanted at having found a woman who gave him a proper son. Fedora seemed almost not to care—"

She didn't pause, apparently unaware of having let slip to Nat, for the first time, a name in this connection.

"—after all, she had kept her part of the bargain. All she cared about was taking her dowry and entering a convent. She said there was another child available, of equally good blood—her own kin, she said—who needed a home. She brought that child to us. Do you think my brother knew one tiny baby from another? And when Laddie grew up looking by some strange whim of God a bit like me—those things happen with adopted children . . . Oh, I knew there was talk of his being my child. You heard some of it yourself, just the other day, at Swank. 'The son of a principessa': they meant me. Even Laddie must have heard it said. I know he wondered. But no, I have never known who she was—or is—that mother. Perhaps Fedora would tell me now. But I won't ask."

Nat almost walked out. Could anything be more despicable than this reason, finally exposed, for the silence at Salerno? To conceal from him, old friend, chronicler of an ancestor, the very existence of this boy whom she had brought up and adored, because he wasn't true "family"? Because he wasn't true "family" she hadn't guarded him more firmly from slipping into Vispo's hands; had been able to stifle her fears until she saw the blond Sicilian die; and to stifle them again when the "family" picture came close. Laddie was loved; but expendable. And he, Nat, had thought Melba's claim to the pictures the most blatant aspect of her madness!

As for himself, Nat immediately felt his affection for Ladislao enhanced. Stripped of all relation to old Deming, both the boy and the affection took on free existence; no longer rooted in the past, they were a breath of new life.

During the next few days, his gratitude for that brought a lessening of his anger at Melba. He was willing to concede that her silence must have been determined by reasons obscure even to herself. There were other elements in the repressions of her life, in the long train of her circumstances, to be added to the ancestor-worship that had provoked his violent reaction.

WHEN IT WAS almost time to go home he moved out of his flat at a month's end and took his old room at the Imperatore. Full summer had come, pool and garden had long since been restored, and Mario was busier than he had been. Nevertheless they had their conversations.

"You may remember, Professore, that morning you had me ask the concierge about the nighttime delivery by the spiderman—I was at work early?"

"You were on the terrace in mufti."

"Supervising repairs. One of my tables and a pair of chairs had been damaged the night before, and the floor tiles badly stained. It was that Signor Vispo. I gathered that a business arrangement with those gentlemen from Rome had come to an end. I heard them reproach him for spending their money too freely— bringing unnecessary people to the island, paying excessive compensation, engaging a string of rooms for those Americans— you know the ones I mean? Signor Vispo was drinking too much and talking too loud, and finally he lost control. He actually lifted a chair in the air and threatened to crash it down on the gentlemen. He did drop it onto the table. Quite a few clients left. The

Carabinieri were called in. But eventually he went upstairs, and the next morning he took the hydrofoil."

"Yes, I saw him leave his room. Has anything been heard of him since?"

"Not to my knowledge. I wonder . . ."

"You wonder what, Mario?"

"It's just that I know who those gentlemen from Rome were, and I saw the way they looked at one another after he went upstairs." Mario was more serious than Nat had seen him. "There's deep salt water between here and Naples."

ON THE EVE OF departure, Nat was talking with Mario about aspects of his stay. It was Mario who had originally urged him to rent the Saccas' upstairs flat, and now he thanked him again for the recommendation. Content though he had eventually been to leave it, the place had worked out well.

"Didn't I tell you it would be nice and quiet for you, Professore? Sacca has those rages, but they're quickly over. And for people with so many family connections, there isn't much coming and going. All the other brothers and sisters went to America, and I don't think you were much bothered by cousins, were you? Sacca and Immacolatina call on them, but not so much the other way round. Everybody knows they like to be left to themselves. They've always been that way."

Mario lowered his voice. "Since you're leaving the island, Professore, and are so discreet anyway, I don't think it can do any harm for me to tell you . . . Sacca and Immacolatina had a bad time once, twenty or so years ago. They'd been careless. Immacolatina was already well along in years, supposedly too late for what happened. She had to disappear for a few months. The child must have been adopted. Everybody knew, nobody asked questions. It happens between brother and sister on this island. This is a pagan place."